SHERL
HOLMES AND THE
HARVEST OF
DEATH

A NARRATIVE BELIEVED TO BE FROM THE PEN OF JOHN H. WATSON, MD

EDITED AND ANNOTATED FOR PUBLICATION BY BARRIE ROBERTS

CHIVERS

British Library Cataloguing in Publication Data available

This Large Print edition published by BBC Audiobooks Ltd, Bath, 2009.
Published by arrangement with the Author's Estate.

U.K. Softcover   ISBN 978 1 408 44137 4

Printed and bound in Great Britain by CPI Antony Rowe, Chippenham
and Eastbourne

Contents

Note

The present text derives from one of a number of manuscripts which have been in the possession of my family for some years. I cannot be certain of their origin, but my maternal grandfather was both a medical man and a contemporary of Watson in the RAMC during the Great War. It is the sixth of the documents which I have edited for publication, the others being *Sherlock Holmes and the Railway Maniac* (Constable, 1994), *Sherlock Holmes and the Devil's Grail* (Constable, 1995), *Sherlock Holmes and the Man from Hell* (Constable, 1997), *Sherlock Holmes and the Royal Flush* (Constable, 1998) and 'The Mystery of the Addleton Curse', which appeared in *The Mammoth Book of New Sherlock Holmes Adventures* (Robinson Books, 1998).

As always, I have sought evidence to establish that this is indeed one of the previously unpublished records of a Sherlock Holmes case, but the proof is difficult, the more so since no unassailable sample of Watson's handwriting is known to exist. The fruits of my researches will be found in the notes at the end of the text and, with such assistance as those give, readers must make up their own minds as to the authenticity of the text. Personally, I am as satisfied as reason permits.

Barrie Roberts

1

A SUMMER MORNING

I was rarely successful in persuading my friend Mr Sherlock Holmes to take a holiday. On many occasions I watched him stretch his prodigious mental and physical abilities to their utmost and always I suggested to him afterwards that a rest, or at the very least a change of air, would help him to recover from his exertions. Mostly my advice passed unheeded. He would take himself off to his room with the cocaine bottle and syringe in the early days of our acquaintance and, even when he had forsworn that vice, he would merely spend a day or two in late rising.

For myself I have long been aware of the recuperative effects of even a few days away from one's accustomed round, and if those days can be passed in the countryside or by the sea, so much the better, but I felt that Holmes resented my absences when I took holidays without him and so I clung to Baker Street long after every sensible mortal with the means had deserted the capital.

Nowadays I hear people complain of the summer weather and compare it unfavourably with the summers they recall from the old Queen's days. Whether their recollection is accurate or dulled by the veil of nostalgia I know not, but my journal shows that the second summer of the century was a long and hot one. The arrest of 'Killer' Evans at midsummer had left me with a slight bullet graze, far from an incapacitating injury but capable of itching furiously as it healed and becoming sore when hot. As a result I was more than ordinarily anxious to leave London's hot and dusty pavements and seek the heaths of the New Forest or the sands of Hayling. Holmes, however, was firmly rooted in London. Indeed, he told me once that his absence from the metropolis provoked an unhealthy unrest among the criminal classes, though he may have been making one of his sly jokes.

London had prepared itself for King Edward's Coronation but his illness had led to a postponement, so that the capital seemed exhausted by the frustrated effort and more so by the weather. The sun rose over the rooftops of Baker Street every morning and, by the time we took our luncheon, was forcing us to draw heavy curtains against its scorching penetration into our little sitting-room.

I tried to breakfast early, while our room was yet cool, but Holmes rarely joined me until I had reached the second pot of tea. One morning in high summer I had completed my meal and was seeking some spot to which the sun would not reach when Holmes finally arrived at the table. He had deferred to the weather sufficiently to abandon his old, nondescript dressing-gown and don a slightly newer garment of silk, though even this was liberally daubed with pipe and cigarette ashes. He gave me a curt greeting and sat himself at the table with his back to the sun, hunching there over a cup of coffee like some great gaudy butterfly that has not yet dried its wings.

I rang for Mrs Hudson and passed Holmes the morning papers while he awaited his breakfast. He leafed through them with an air of distaste.

'There is not sufficient here,' he complained, 'to engage Scotland Yard, let alone to warrant the services of a consulting detective.'

I nodded. 'Everyone has gone to the country, to the seaside, or abroad,' I said. 'I cannot help thinking that we might be wise to follow them.'

He stared at me for a moment. 'Watson,' he said, 'I do not have your capacity to regenerate myself among scenes bucolic or maritime. I need to exercise my brain cells, to come to grips with a problem of such singularity that it forces me to focus my entire capacity upon it.' He waved a dismissive hand at the newspapers. 'If one believes the public prints, one can only infer that not only society and the middle classes are on holiday, but also every criminal in this broad city.'

Mrs Hudson entered with his breakfast, but

he merely picked at it, a sure sign that he was in dire need of excitement.

'Come, Holmes,' I said, 'how many times have I heard you voice the same complaint, only to find that within minutes there was a client at our door?' I deemed it necessary to try and distract him, being ever aware of the cocaine bottle.

'Hah!' he snorted. 'I have had clients in recent days, Watson, as well you know. And what have they brought me? Elementary exercises in the tracing of missing relatives, or simple recovery of stolen property. I have remarked before, Watson, that I believed I had touched bottom, that I had degenerated into an agency for recovering lost pencils and giving advice to young ladies from boarding schools—well, if it was not so then it is so now!'

I had no adequate reply to this sally, but was, in any case, forestalled by the return of Mrs Hudson.

'I know you're still about your breakfast, Mr Holmes,' she said, 'but there's a young man downstairs who wishes to see you most urgently—a very respectable young man,' she emphasised.

'A complete lack of respectability might be a better passport,' commented Holmes. 'No doubt he has come about a lost dog, but show him up, Mrs Hudson, show him up!'

She cleared away Holmes' almost

4

untouched breakfast and, in a very few minutes, introduced the caller as 'Mr Russell.'

He was a tall, fair young man in his twenties who wore his hair cut short in a military fashion and was dressed in a plain suit and solid well-polished boots. He stood at the door with his right hand held behind his back and the left arm slightly crooked at his side. I took him to be an ex-soldier.

'I'm sorry, gentlemen, to disturb you so early in the day,' he said with his eyes upon Holmes' dressing-gown, 'but the business that brought me to London is completed and I must soon be on my way home. Still, I could not resist the opportunity to ask your advice upon a matter that has been troubling me.'

Holmes smiled. 'Pray take the basket chair, Constable,' he said. 'And tell us about the matter that troubles you.'

The young man started then recovered himself and took the offered seat. 'I do not know how you knew I am a police officer,' he said. 'I never mentioned it to the lady downstairs.'

Holmes smiled again. 'You are easily over six feet tall,' he said, 'and you carry yourself like a man accustomed to uniform. Your clothing shows little sign of wear and may be that of a man who more usually wears a uniform, all of which, of course, might make you a soldier but you do not stand easy nor at attention—you stand with a hand behind the

5

back and, since your hat is no doubt in the care of Mrs Hudson, with your left arm crooked as though your helmet lay in it. It is the characteristic pose of a constable in the witness box. If I wanted confirmation, your accent reveals that you have come from somewhere in the vicinity of Berkshire or Wiltshire and have travelled this morning by train, escorting a prisoner to London—the mark of the handcuff is still on your left wrist.'

It was our visitor's turn to smile though a little nervously. 'I had hoped, sir, that you was as good as the newspapers say, and I have to say that you are.'

Honest praise always warmed my friend. 'You are too generous, Constable,' he said. 'I have merely trained myself to be observant of little things, for they tend to matter most of all. Now, to your problem.'

'I am,' began our guest, 'a police constable, as you rightly deduced, Mr Holmes. I have been in the service seven years and, though perhaps I says it as shouldn't, I hope I knows my duties and obligations properly by now.' He paused. 'What is more, sir, I not only try to do all that is rightly required of me, but I will not have any truck with those in the force who are inclined to conceal each other's misdeeds. That way, I believe, lies wickedness and I was brought up to do what is right.'

He thrust his jaw slightly forward, as though inviting us to take issue with his proposition, but Holmes nodded.

'Your attitude does you credit, Constable, but I suspect that it may make matters between yourself and your colleagues awkward on some occasions.'

'Perhaps it did once, Mr Holmes,' the young man replied, 'but I have made myself plain to my fellows for the seven years as I have served and I think they understand now that if they wants someone to turn a blind eye, then I am not their man. What is more, my sergeant—that is Sergeant Bullington—is a man with the same view. He was twenty years in the Army, mostly in India, before he joined the force, and until recently he was always one for doing things straight and according to the book.'

'Recently?' said Holmes. 'He has, then, changed his attitude?'

The young constable seemed distressed. 'This is not an easy thing to do, Mr Holmes. Sergeant Bullington is my superior officer and it goes against the grain to complain of him, the more so since he has always supported my own attitude and has taken pains to see to my training.'

He clenched his hands and twisted them nervously. 'Until a short while ago,' he continued, 'I would have said as Sergeant Bullington never said a wrong word or put a foot wrong, but a matter has arisen which has caused me to question his actions. I dare not take it over his head, partly because they would likely not believe me and partly because I cannot help believing that a man like the sergeant must have had a sound reason for what he has done. I have lost sleep over this affair and, when I was told off to deliver a prisoner to London, it occurred to me that here was an opportunity to consult yourself and see what you might make of it.'

'I see,' said Holmes. 'Now, Constable, in what way has the sergeant so completely altered his attitude as to cause you to lose sleep?'

'Oh, his attitude, sir, is as before—everything up to the mark and properly done. But in this one thing he has behaved in a way that I cannot understand—in a manner which I do not think right in any police officer.'

'What is this singular instance, Constable?'

He twisted his hands again. 'Why, Mr Holmes, I was present when the sergeant received a confession of murder, and not only did he take no action, he released the man as made it and ordered me to say nothing about it.'

'Did he?' said Holmes, and his eyes glittered. 'That is, indeed, remarkable. Watson, pray ring for Mrs Hudson. Let us have more tea while this young man continues his story.'

2

A CONFESSION OF MURDER

When tea had been served Holmes leaned back in his chair and slowly rubbed his right palm with his left thumb. I knew it for a sign that he expected stimulation from our visitor's narrative and I was pleased to see it.

'Now, Constable Russell,' he said, 'let us hear about Sergeant Bullington's lapse. You are not giving evidence before a court here, so let us have what you think and what you believe, as well as what you know.'

The young man nodded and took a long, thoughtful draught of his tea. Then he narrowed his eyes as though concentrating his recollection.

'Well, sir,' he began, 'it occurred towards the time of the hay harvest.'

'That would be June, I think,' said Holmes.

'A little earlier, sir, towards the end of May. We has good weather as a rule in our parts and the harvest tends to come a little earlier than in counties farther west or north. A lot of the harvest gangs starts their year's work with us. I recall that it was after Whitsun,' he went on, 'because the party in question had appeared in the village at Whitsun.'

'Which was the village?' asked Holmes.

Russell drank his tea again. 'I had been told off to assist Sergeant Bullington at Weston Stacey. That's a little place, sir—not much more than a village—in the west of the county. The duty there is not very hard as there is little that you might call crime, and in the ordinary way Sergeant Bullington would deal with it easy with one constable, but he had been unwell and if truth is told I believe the years are beginning to tell on him so the superintendent over at Hardbourne, he decided as the sergeant should have an experienced constable to assist him and I was assigned.'

'Had you any specific duties,' asked Holmes, 'or were they general?'

'Oh, I was just generally to assist the sergeant and to work to his orders, sir. Sometimes I would walk the beat with the sergeant or with the probationer, Constable Wilkes, or by myself. At other times I would keep the desk at the station and attend to the paperwork. As I said, sir, it was not arduous duty and I was pleased to be working once more under a man who I truly believed to be the very model of what a policeman should be.

'Now at Weston Stacey they make a great deal of Whitsun. They has a walk by all the little girls all dressed in white and they keeps up a proper Whitsun Ale on the green with stalls and shies and bowling for pigs and that. There's other villages where the parson won't allow it, but Reverend Trentham is a kindly sort of man and he says it's right as people should want to celebrate the coming of summer and he says it's all right so long as the credit is given where 'tis due.

'So this year they was having the Whitsun Ale, which does give us a little bit of bother. Not from the Weston people—the worst they does is drink too much and fall over in a ditch—but you get strangers from villages roundabout and from the town and they can be troublesome sometimes, fighting and that. Now this year I was keeping an eye on things on the green and I seen this party making a nuisance of himself.'

'In what way?' said Holmes.

'Well, sir, he'd had more than enough to drink for a start, but that wasn't it. I noticed particular as he'd spy out a good-looking young girl on her own and he'd slide in alongside her—maybe at one of the stalls or the shies where she might be standing to watch. He wouldn't have stood by her long when she'd move away sharpish, and I thought to myself, "He's making himself unwelcome."'

'What did you do?' asked Holmes.

'Well, Mr Holmes, as luck would have it he fell into an argument with one of the local lads and it looked as if it might come to blows. So I stepped up quickly and I took aholt of this party by the collar. "What's adoing here?" I said and young Wilf Harness—that was him as

11

he had been arguing with—he said, "He's been annoying my Maisie while I was bowling and I'm going to see to him." "No you don't, Wilf Harness," I said, "you see to your Maisie and I'll look after this fellow," and I took him by the scruff and marched him off.'

'What manner of person was he?' enquired Holmes.

'What manner of person?' repeated the policeman. 'He was forty or more, I would say, and from the country. Folks dress up a bit for the Whitsun Ale, but he was poorly dressed, shabby like in what looked like working clothes and a greasy old billycock.'

'Why do you say he was a countryman?'

'Well, Mr Holmes, his face was paler than a country-bred chap's, but he had his trousers tied about like a farm-hand. I thought as he might be a haymaker, come to get work on the harvest, one as had been out of employment and had not had his face weathered for a while.'

'Or one who had been in prison?' suggested Holmes.

The young man nodded. 'Yes, sir. That might be true though it never crossed my mind at the time.'

'Go on with your story,' said Holmes.

'Well, sir, as I say, I took him off to the lock-up meaning to leave him there overnight so as he wouldn't be a nuisance to anyone else during the Ales. He didn't give me no trouble, just went along with me quiet and never even asked what I was taking him for. So I took him to the lock-up and told the probationer constable to see him locked up for the night then I went back to the green.'

He gazed into his empty teacup and then eyed the pot, so I replenished his cup, After a long swallow he carried on.

'I thought no more about him, sir, until the next morning. I was just arriving at the station and Sergeant Bullington was at the desk. He had this fellow out of his cell and was giving him a good talking to before he sent him away. He believes in that, does the sergeant, reckons that being locked up should be of some moral purpose to the offender.

'Seeing as the sergeant was busy, I just wished him a good morning and went through to the back office. It was while I was in there that I heard the conversation that passed between the sergeant and the prisoner.'

'And what was that?' said Holmes.

'Well, sir, at first Sergeant Bullington was giving him a talking-to about letting the drink get the better of him and lead him into evil ways. I wasn't listening to that especially, because I'd heard it often enough before, but then the prisoner began to cry. Even in the back room I could hear him sobbing out loud like a child. And that's when he said it, sir.'

'What, as precisely as you can recall, did the prisoner say?'

'Well, I thought at first as he was having a weep the way those recovering from drink often does, but then I heard him repeating the same words. In between his sobbing he kept on saying, "But I let them kill her, Sergeant—I let them kill her. I didn't do nothing to stop it," and again he'd say, "She was a pretty little lass and they killed her like a rabbit."'

Holmes' eyes were fixed on the young man's face. 'You are sure,' he said, 'that you heard those precise words? You cannot have misheard, have been mistaken in any way?'

The constable shook his head. 'No, sir, for he said them over and over.'

'And how did your sergeant respond?'

'Well, sir, that's what I cannot understand. Here was this fellow saying as someone had been killed, a little lass, and that he might have prevented it, and I fully expected the sergeant to take him up on it—to want particulars and all, but he didn't. He just said to him, "Look here, my man, you can get yourself into a good deal of trouble with saying things like that. You might find yourself up at Salisbury Assizes and them as did it wouldn't be there with you. You'd be hanged alone for what others did. You'd be better off to stay away from the drink, get yourself some lawful employment and not to be seen in these parts again."'

'Is there,' asked Holmes, 'the least possibility that you are mistaken as to the conversation that you heard?'

14

'No, sir,' said Constable Russell. 'The man himself was almost shouting, and although he was sobbing in between the words I heard them clearly. As to Sergeant Bullington, he has a commanding voice, you might say.'

My friend nodded. 'Pray continue,' he said.

'Well, Mr Holmes, I didn't know at all what to make of all this, but I wouldn't have the sergeant believe that I was spying on him, so I walked out to the front desk. Sergeant Bullington was sat on the high stool at the desk with the Occurrences Book open in front of him and the prisoner was stood up in front of the desk. He had both hands on the edge of the desk like he was clutching on to it and his face was dropped down on his hands.'

Russell paused in his narrative and dropped his face to indicate how the man had held his head. 'He wasn't talking no more, Mr Holmes. He was just sobbing and weeping. When he raised his head there was great tears running down his dirty face.'

'Well, the sergeant saw me and he says, "Russell, this man is as sober as I care to wait for. Escort him to the parish boundary," he says, "and make him understand that he's not to be seen in these parts again." So I takes the man by the elbow and I steers him into the street, and just as we're passing out of the police station door, Sergeant Bullington calls after us. He says, "Dazzy Cooke, you mind what I said and you keep away from the drink or you'll fetch up at a rope's end!" '

'Dazzy Cooke,' repeated Holmes. 'You are positive that was the name the sergeant used?'

'Oh yes, sir. I made a particular note of it in my head, because by that time I was fair puzzled as to what was going forward. Anyway, sir, I took the fellow, as I'd been ordered, and I walked him to the boundary, and all the time he kept heaving great sighs and shaking his head, but he never addressed any word to me. Not until we reached the Salisbury milestone that marks the boundary. I let go his elbow there and I said a few stern words to him about not coming back to Weston Stacey or he'd face Sergeant Bullington's wrath. Then he looked me in the face and he said, "Oh no, Constable. I shan't be back in Weston Stacey and I shan't face Sergeant Bullington's wrath. I shall go elsewhere until I has to face a greater wrath." With that he turns away and I stood by the milestone and watched him out of sight.'

'And has he been seen again in your parish?' asked my friend. The constable shook his head. 'No, sir,' he said.

'And has Sergeant Bullington vouchsafed you any explanation of the matter?'

'He's not one for explaining his actions to his subordinates, sir, but when I come back to the station I did mention the matter. I said that the man had seemed to be very upset. Sergeant Bullington only said, "Drink, Russell —the effects of drink. The morning after they see their sins more clearly than they likes and it makes some of them tearful," and with that he told me off to other duties.'

'And have you heard no more of the matter?' I asked.

'No, Doctor,' he said. 'I took the opportunity of looking at the Occurrences Book as soon as I might but Sergeant Bullington had not even entered in the man's particulars and the fact of his being kept in a cell overnight.'

'Which is most irregular,' commented Holmes.

'Indeed, sir. In fact it is the only time I have known Sergeant Bullington depart from the proper way of doing things.'

Holmes sat back and steepled his long fingers before his face.

'So, Constable,' he said, 'we have a long-serving police sergeant, a man of the best character and a stickler for the proper procedures. This man hears what seems to be a confession to complicity in murder and, so far from taking the usual actions, has the confessor removed from the parish with a stern warning to keep silent, then fails to make any record at all of the incident. I can understand your concern, Constable. It is indeed singular.'

The young policeman nodded.

'Tell me,' continued Holmes. 'Is there, in fact, an unsolved murder of a girl that you know of in your area?'

'Yes, sir. There is. Little Bea Collins was

17

murdered last summer and the matter remains a mystery.'

'Ah!' exclaimed Holmes. 'I think you had better tell us about the death of Bea Collins.'

3

THE DEATH OF BEATRICE COLLINS

'You must understand, Mr Holmes, that I do not have all the particulars of the death of Beatrice Collins, it being as she was not from Weston Stacey. But I was concerned in the search for her and I saw her body where it was found.'

Holmes nodded. 'When did her death occur?' he asked.

'Last summer,' said the constable. 'Just as the harvest was ending. I remember the last load had gone home from Toadneck Manor the day she went missing, and that night was the Harvest Supper. I was there when the sergeant sent word to me to get together a party to search for her.'

'How old was she?' asked my friend. 'And in what circumstances did she go missing?'

'She was ten, sir. She was the oldest child of old Fetchy Collins—Fletcher Collins is his right name. He's a useless article, sir. He does a bit of hedging and ditching and casual work, but he's much given to drinking, sir and he has a wife and six little ones—seven before poor little Bea was killed. They lives in a cottage at Buckstone, that's a little hamlet west of the village. The cottage is an horrible broken-down sort of place. Still, Mrs Collins keeps her children clean and well behaved. We never has trouble with the Collins boys like with other families.'

'Are the survivors all boys?' interjected Holmes.

'Yes, sir,' said Russell. 'Little Bea was her only daughter, a pretty, bright little girl, well thought of by everyone and hard-working like her brothers. They must get it from their mother. It certainly don't come from old Fetchy.'

'And the circumstances of her death?' prompted my friend.

'Like I said, sir, it was harvest end—the day of the Harvest Feast. Now I don't know if you gentlemen understand how the harvest is brought in. To make sure as all the crop comes in while the weather holds, each farmer lets his men work on other farms until his corn is ready and the big farms, they hires harvest masters to bring in gangs of labour to help out—chaps from other parts of the country, where the harvest is already in or hasn't started yet, earning a bit of extra. So there's a lot of moving about, of people being where they aren't usually and strangers about and that. Added to which, the last fields to be harvested are always the manor farm, that's by old custom, sir.'

'And Toadneck Manor is the manor farm in your area?' said Holmes.

'That's right, Mr Holmes. So last year it was the last day of harvesting, and everyone was at Toadneck Manor. That's the men and women from the farms about, the harvest gangs and the children.'

'Children?' queried Holmes.

The constable nodded. 'The children,' he repeated. 'Of course, the parents aren't supposed to do it, to hold the little ones from school to work, but they does it just the same. They holds them from school at the hay harvest and, of course, it isn't usually school time when the corn harvest comes in, so that's all right.'

'What sort of age are these children?' I asked.

He shook his head, sadly. 'Very young, Doctor, very young. The harvest masters will hire kiddies of six or seven years to fetch and carry and glean in the fields and pay them only a few pence. Most times they have to labour from early morning until twilight and sometimes they has to walk three, four or five miles to get to their work and back again after.'

'And little Bea Collins was one such?' asked Holmes.

'That's right, sir. Old Fetchy had hired her to a harvest master called Platt. Platt's a regular in our parts, comes up from Dorset in the season, hay and corn harvests he comes. Well, little Bea was working with his gang first at Buckstone Farm then at Sixwells, but that last day all the gangs was at Toadneck Manor and it being the Feast day there was a lot going on.'

'What manner of thing was going on?' asked Holmes.

'Well, sir, if it's been a good harvest and not rushed nor delayed by the weather, the last day is a bit of a celebration, sir. In the first place there's every available hand there from all about. Then, at dinner-time, the womenfolk puts on their best and brightest when they brings the dinner out to the fields to their men and stays with them while they has their dinner. They likes to put a bit of something special in the basin for the men, too—a bit of lardy cake or a bit of jam pastry, something like that, and the men sees as there's a few little treats for the children. Then, after they've eaten there's usually a bit of a sing-song before they turns back to work—old songs, like "John Barleycorn" and "The Jolly Wagoner" and that.'

'And this little celebration took place at Toadneck Manor last year?'

'Oh yes, sir. 'Twas a fair harvest and there was plenty to be pleased about.'

'And Beatrice Collins was among the children at Toadneck Manor at that dinner-time?'

'Yes, sir. She was remembered because she sung a song. But she was not there later when the neck was cried.'

'I beg your pardon?' said Holmes. 'When the neck was cried?'

'It's the custom, sir. The last bunch of corn is called the "goose's neck". The reapers throws their sickles at it till it is cut and when it is cut there is a bit of chanting and ceremony. The reapers form two lines and the man with the neck runs out of the field between them. Well, there was no one who could recall seeing little Bea in the harvest field then.'

'And what happens after the neck has gone from the field?' I asked. I had spent much of my boyhood in a rural county but had never heard of this strange custom.

'It goes—well, it goes to the farm, sir. It hangs up at the Harvest Feast and it is kept until next year. Some farmers mixes the grains from it with the seed-corn at the next planting.'

Holmes nodded. 'I have seen something similar in the Isle of Skye,' he said. 'There, when a farmer finishes his harvest, he sends a sheaf to a farmer who has not yet finished. They call that sheaf the *goabbir bhacagh*—the crippled goat. But we digress. You say that Bea Collins was not present as the neck left the field?'

'That's right, sir.'

'And where would she have gone in the

22

usual way of things?'

'Well, sir, once the neck has gone the last cart is loaded and goes home to the farm. Those as is going to the Feast either goes with it, or they goes home to dress for the Feast.'

'And the children?'

'Some of the older ones would be going to the Feast. They'd as like ride on the last wagon. The others would just go on home. Little Bea wasn't going to the Feast. Old Fetchy would never have let her. He was going, of course, though he'd never lifted a hand in the harvest, but Mrs Collins and the children was to stay at home.'

'So the children not going to the Feast would have left the field after the last wagon?'

The young man nodded. 'Yes, sir,' he said. 'Though nobody recalls seeing little Bea leave.'

'The harvest master,' I said, 'this man Platt—does he have no responsibility for seeing his child-labourers safely home?'

Russell smiled at the idea. 'Not him, Doctor. He's just responsible for seeing they does their work. It's the parents' place to get them to the fields and home again.'

'And how far is Toadneck Farm from Bea Collins' home at Buckstone?' asked Holmes.

'Two—maybe two and a half miles.'

'And when was she missed?'

'That'd be late on. I had the evening off duty and I was at the Feast with everyone else.

23

It was after dark, the lanterns was lit and the singing had been going on some while. Mrs Collins come with the probationer constable. She'd walked in from Buckstone when Bea didn't come home by dusk and told the sergeant. He sent her with the probationer for me with a message to start up a search at once.'

'And she was not on the road from Toadneck to Buckstone?'

'No, sir. Mrs Collins and the probationer had walked all that way and they never saw her.'

'And what action did you take?'

'With help from Mr Grainger—he's the farmer at Toadneck—I got search parties out with torches and we quartered the country about, between Toadneck and Buckstone. It wasn't easy. It was pitchy dark by then and we'd all had a good deal too much to eat and a bit too much to drink but we had to do it.'

'And what result did you obtain?'

'We'd been out maybe two hours—it would have been about midnight—when I heard a shout from Mr Grainger's party. They was near the Mayfield, that's a field about half-way from Buckstone to Toadneck. When we got there, they'd found her. She was laid down beside the path across the field on her back with her eyes open like a little doll and she was dead.'

He paused and Holmes waited a moment

before prompting him.

'How had she died?' he asked at last.

'She had been hit and she'd been strangled, sir. She was hit once and then choked, poor little lass.'

4

A SINGULAR WEAPON

Holmes knocked out his pipe on the fender and began to refill it from the Persian slipper where he kept his tobacco.

'With what had she been strangled?' he asked.

Constable Russell shook his head. 'We never knew,' he said. The surgeon said as she'd been strangled with something like a neckerchief or a scarf but it wasn't where her body was.'

'And at harvest time,' said Holmes, 'all of the men and youths working in the fields would be wearing neckerchiefs to keep the dust from their necks. Were any of them missing their kerchiefs?'

'No, sir. The surgeon—Dr Ryall—said that the cloth that done it would be stretched and creased with the force used, so we looked at everyone's neck-cloths but there was no telling, sir. Some had worn them in the field all day and they was creased all ways; some had put fresh ones on for the Feast so they weren't creased.'

'So Dr Ryan's point led nowhere,' said Holmes. 'Nevertheless, in cases of strangulation by a cloth, the weapon is almost always an item of clothing—if not from the victim, from the murderer. On the evidence of your inspection, she might well have been killed by one of those who left the harvest field to return home and change their clothing. If it had been done on the way home, they might have returned to the Feast with a fresh neckerchief.'

He thought for a moment, his head flung back and his eyes half closed, then, 'What was Dr Ryall's view of the time of her death?' he asked.

'As near as he could put it, he said early in the evening, maybe six or seven o'clock.'

'And at what time was the neck cried at the farm?'

'That was about six, sir.'

'I see,' said Holmes. 'So it appears that the child—who was not recalled as present when the neck was cried—had made her way home at about that time and was waylaid.' He dropped his head forwards. 'Would her usual way home have taken her near or through the Mayfield where she was found?'

'The Mayfield is a field that lies on top of a little rise, Mr Holmes. Coming from Toadneck, the lane runs around the bottom of it through

26

Buckstone, which is on the far side from Toadneck Farm. There is a path across the Mayfield, but that would have taken her out of her way.'

'She had younger brothers, you say. Were any of them at Toadneck Farm and what did they recall?'

'Two of her brothers was at Toadneck with the harvest gang. They was gleaning, so they stayed on the field after it was cut and the wagon had gone. They didn't go home until it was falling dark and they couldn't see to glean any longer, but they thought little Bea had gone ahead and they didn't think nothing about it until they got home and she wasn't there.'

Holmes nodded, thoughtfully. 'So, it seems likely that she was abducted on her way home at about six in the evening—at a time when everyone was concerned with the business of the last sheaf and so on. Did your enquiries reveal anyone else to have left the field at that time or earlier?'

'No, sir. We took particular care to check who was there. All them as reported for work stayed to the end apart from Bea Collins and a couple of other little ones. Mr Grainger, the farmer, came down to the field at dinner-time and stayed till the last wagon. Mr Trentham— the vicar—he came along in the morning to say a prayer before the cutting began but he didn't stay. His niece as lives with him wasn't

27

there—no, I tell a lie—it was haymaking when she was away. She was there at harvesting, she came down with some of the reapers' wives at dinner-time and she stayed a while but she'd gone when the neck was cried. She thinks that sort of thing is not quite Christian.'

Holmes nodded again. 'So when Bea Collins left the harvest field there would have been no one to see her on her way to Buckstone—no one, that is, save her murderer?'

'That's right, Mr Holmes. Every able-bodied man was at the field, all the wives, and even the children that wasn't working was there to see the fun.'

'You were unable to trace the cloth that strangled her but you said that she had also been struck. Did you find the weapon? Was it a branch? A stone? A cudgel?'

'No, Mr Holmes. That was another mystery. I should have expected the injury to be from such as you have mentioned, but it was not. Dr Ryall said as she had been hit sharp on the head so as to leave a little hole with an implement of some kind. He described it as having a rectangular cross-section and tapering to a point. He thought that it was probably of metal, but no one seemed to be able to think of such an item, whether a weapon or a tool.'

'The blade of a chisel?' I suggested.

'Dr Ryall said not, sir. He said it didn't have a cutting end or edge, it had a sort of squared point, tapering from about a half-inch wide.'

'A cordwainer's punch?' suggested Holmes. 'They use many differently shaped implements in punching holes into leather.'

The young man's face brightened. 'We never considered that, sir. I imagine something like that may be a possibility.'

'And it may be,' said my friend, 'that a number of persons connected with the harvest would carry such an implement if they needed to adjust or repair the leather belts of agricultural machinery. I do not imagine that there are many such men in your village. Not many labourers are skilled with machinery.'

Constable Russell looked encouraged. 'We shall need to pay attention to those men who do tinker with the farm machines,' he said.

'Indeed,' said Holmes, 'but remember that I have merely advanced a theory as to the nature of the weapon. It might equally have been a bookbinder's tool, though I doubt that such would be as common in the country and even a cordwainer's punch would be a singular weapon.'

The young officer looked crestfallen. 'How many times had she been struck, and whereabouts?' continued Holmes.

'There was just the one blow, sir. To the back of her head. Dr Ryall said that it would very likely have stunned her and then she was strangled.'

'And was there any indication of a disturbance, a struggle, any signs that she had

29

attempted to escape from her killer?'

'None whatsoever, sir. She was laid on her back beside the path across the Mayfield with her hands clasped in front of her, holding a corn dolly.'

'A corn dolly?' queried Holmes.

I recalled them from my country childhood. 'A plaited decoration,' I said, 'made from corn strands and ears and kept as a charm. You will see them in country inns hanging from the beams.'

'Of course,' said Holmes. 'So it appears that the child went willingly into the Mayfield, with some person whom she trusted or from whom she feared no harm. There she was struck once with a pointed implement, rendering her senseless, and then she was strangled.'

'That's right,' said Russell.

'Was there any sign of any indecency having occurred?'

The constable shook his head firmly. 'None at all,' he said.

Holmes steepled his fingers and gazed over them. 'A penniless child cannot have been killed for gain. She was not, ostensibly, the victim of a moral defective, nor can her death have been in any way self-defence. What do you make of it, Watson?'

'Might she have been the victim of another child?' I hazarded.

'No, sir,' said Constable Russell. 'It was Dr Ryall's belief that the blow that stunned her was a fierce blow, struck from behind and above most likely by an adult or a tall youth.'

'Then I am at a loss,' I said.

'And so, for the time being, am I,' admitted Holmes. 'You and your colleagues have found no further clue in the twelve months since?'

'No, sir. Not a trace nor a whisper.'

'And there has been no repetition, or no further such attempt?'

'No, sir.'

'You associate this poor child's death with the apparent confession of the drunkard,' said Holmes. 'Why is that?'

'Well, sir, he spoke of a little lass and there is no other little lass whose death remains unsolved in our area.'

'But he was, in your experienced view, a harvest labourer. If he follows the gangs he might have referred to a matter which took place anywhere, from Land's End to John o'Groat's. Has he, by the way, been seen in your vicinity since the death of Bea Collins?'

The young man looked crestfallen again. 'No, sir. He hasn't. But, Mr Holmes, if what that man was saying meant nothing to the sergeant—if he was talking about Land's End or John o'Groat's—why did Sergeant Bullington send him on his way, without enquiry, sir? I can't escape the feeling that the sergeant knew what the man was talking about. He spoke to him of hanging at Salisbury, and that would make it our area, sir, would it not?'

31

'Excellent points, Constable, and, for the lack of further data, we must take account of your impressions.' Holmes drew his watch from his pocket and consulted it. 'We have kept you too long, Constable. You have a long journey in front of you but you shall hear from me shortly. Watson here has been urging upon me the advantages of a visit to the country. Is there a reasonable inn at Weston Stacey?'

'Mr Garrett keeps a good house at the John Barleycorn, sir. Would you wish me to reserve rooms for you?'

'No, thank you, Constable. I think Weston Stacey had better not see us as Sherlock Holmes and Dr Watson. Watson's little fables have made us too well known to operate with the necessary freedom on occasions. We shall make contact with you in some other guise. In the meantime, say nothing to anyone of your visit here today, or of your misgivings about your sergeant.'

When our door had closed behind the young man I smiled at Holmes. 'So we are bound for the West Country,' I said.

'Indeed,' said Holmes, 'and be sure to pack your Adams .450.'

'For the country—really, Holmes! What are we dealing with here?'

'I do not know, Watson, I do not know, but unless some simple explanation eludes me, we may be venturing into deep waters—deep waters, indeed.'

5

A SUMMER VACATION

Holmes might see our journey as beset by unspoken dangers, but I could not resist a certain lightness of mood as we boarded our train at Paddington the next morning. Events had conspired to drive Holmes out of London and I proposed, while fully supporting his enquiry in any way which he required of me, to take advantage of this providential change of circumstances. Nevertheless, in accordance with my friend's warning, my Adams .450 lay loaded in the top of my suitcase.

I cannot estimate the thousands of miles of railway over which he and I travelled in the quarter of a century during which I was associated with Sherlock Holmes. In our last and longest enquiry alone—the affair of the Railway Maniac—we pursued our enquiries from London to Plymouth, Salisbury, Grantham, Aberdeen and Hampshire. [See *Sherlock Holmes and the Railway Maniac*, Constable, 1994.] In all those journeyings I could never predict the mood of my travelling companion. On occasions he would sit for hours in silence, on others he would converse freely and cheerfully about the wonderfully wide range of topics that exercised his curiosity and occasionally, though rarely, he would discuss the case in hand.

It was that last mood which I recognised as we drew out of Paddington's soot-shrouded gloom into the bright sunlight of yet another sweltering day. My friend, as I have often remarked, was unimpressed with the virtues of fresh air, but as the full force of the morning sun struck our carriage he stepped to the window and carefully adjusted the sliding ventilator panels then relaxed into his seat, reaching for his pipe.

'Yesterday,' I remarked, 'it would have taken a wagon and horses to drag you away to the country. Now, here we are on our way west.'

'You will have noticed,' he replied, 'that I made a point of absenting myself from London at the time when King Edward's Coronation was first due to occur. For reasons that seem sufficient to me, I would prefer that my brother Mycroft should be unaware of my whereabouts until His Majesty is crowned.'

'Oh come,' I joked. 'Surely you will not risk the Government needing your assistance and being unable to call upon you?'

'Parliament,' he said, 'is in recess.' The Lords and Commons have gone to the shires or back to their constituencies. The Civil Service are largely on holiday. The press is deep into what Fleet Street itself calls the "silly season" and the criminals of London have decamped to the seaside. I doubt if His Majesty's Government cannot rub along without me for a day or two. Besides, the tale which Constable Russell has told us promises a singular investigation. You have, I hope, followed my advice and brought your revolver?'

'I have,' I said. 'Why do you believe that this is a dangerous enquiry? All we have at present is the senseless murder of a poor village child and the seeming confession of a drunkard.'

'We have also,' he reminded me, 'the extraordinary conduct of Sergeant Bullington, and it is the very senselessness that concerns me, Watson. Murder—whether of adults or children—is never lacking in its own rationality. The murder of children is almost an English disease, but in most cases the reasons are simple. Parents destroy their offspring out of drunken brutality or in response to a degree of poverty that has driven them mad. Strangers who kill children almost always do so in gratification of some monstrous urge or, having inflicted some moral outrage upon the child, to ensure its silence. The death of Beatrice Collins falls into none of these categories.'

'And you are positive that she was not the victim of such a lunatic?' I asked.

'Look,' he said, 'at the manner of her death. Taken into the Mayfield by some person or persons in whom she trusted or from whom she feared no harm—'

'You said that yesterday,' I interrupted, 'but I do not entirely understand your certainty on the point.'

'Constable Russell explained to us that the Mayfield lies adjacent to the child's road home to Buckstone, but that the path across it would have led her away from her home.'

'True,' I agreed, 'but might she not have wandered aside to play in the Mayfield?'

'Indeed she might, Watson, and I amend my conclusions accordingly, but my basic point remains—when confronted by her killer or killers she saw no reason for fear.'

'Very well,' I said, pleased that I had made a small point, 'but what then?'

'Then,' he said, 'for what reason we know not, she was struck from behind with the singular instrument which Dr Ryall indicated.'

'The cordwainer's punch?'

'Watson! Watson!' he chided. 'The wound, as described by Constable Russell, was not so distinctive as to leave no doubt about the weapon with which it was inflicted. That it may have been a leather punch was no more than a suggestion. It might equally have been a gold-embosser's tool or any one of fifty implements employed in different trades. It is of the utmost importance, in the early stages of an investigation, to distinguish between what is fact, what is reasonable speculation based upon the facts and what is unreasonable speculation that has no connection with the facts. You have confused the first and second.'

'Very well,' I said. 'She was struck from behind with some curious weapon, a blow which Dr Ryall thought would have rendered her unconscious.'

Holmes nodded. 'At this point one must ask why that attack ceased. If, as you suggest, she was the victim of a lunatic, then there are only a limited number of possibilities. If her attacker was of that peculiarly morbid variety whose satisfaction lies in the act of murder itself then one must ask why, having struck her senseless and having in hand a weapon capable of inflicting deadly injury, the murderer did not complete his work by battering her about the head until she died?'

I saw the force of his reasoning and forbore to interrupt.

'On the other hand,' he continued, 'whereas the blow to the head might have been intended to disable her so as to permit her murderer to take indecent advantage of her, we know that no such assault occurred. Had it done, the facts would speak clearly—that the attacker stunned her with a blow, carried out his intentions and then strangled her to prevent her making an identification or giving a description. That is not what occurred in the Mayfield. It is almost as though she were stunned so that she could be strangled without resistance.'

'That must be right,' I said.

He looked perplexed. 'It is what the facts suggest, Watson, but it makes little sense. It implies that the murder of Bea Collins was directed by some personal animus against her, that she was lured into the Mayfield, or ambushed there, by some person or persons who wished to kill her specifically.'

'Why does that make no sense?'

'Because, Watson, she was the ten-year-old child of a poor labourer. If murder is not driven by lust or madness, it arises from greed, fear or revenge. What did she have? Why should anyone fear her? What might she have done to provoke such a dreadful revenge? No, Watson, there is a singularity about the death of Bea Collins that bodes ill for Weston Stacey.'

'You believe there will be another killing or killings? But it has been a year since her death.'

'If the motive of a killer can be identified, Watson, it is normally a short step to the identification of the perpetrator. Where a killing occurs out of madness or for some deeply secret motive it is far harder to name the murderer. All that can safely be said at present is that Bea Collins met her death at the hands of a person or persons who either lives in or visits the area and has a concealed motive which led to the act. Whether that motive might lead to further murders it is impossible to say. Only the killer or killers could answer that question.'

He applied himself to loading his pipe while I considered his analysis. I admit that I still believed the child's death might have arisen from some form of madness which was as yet undefined and which had defeated Holmes' logic.

When my friend's pipe was drawing to his satisfaction he settled in the corner of the compartment, staring unseeingly out of the window. A query had occurred to me and I hastened to make it, for I knew that he was capable of lapsing into ruminative silences that might stretch for hours.

'I note,' I remarked, 'that you refer to the possibility that there was more than one killer. Is that what you believe?'

'I believe only what is revealed by the facts, Watson.'

'But there is no evidence of more than one killer, Holmes.'

'The two separate attacks, with a striking weapon and a strangling cloth, may be such evidence, Watson. What is more, if Constable Russell is right in his suspicions about the harvest labourer, then his remarks imply more than one.'

'I noted yesterday that you did not question the officer as to the indications at the scene of the crime. You are usually very interested in footprints and the like.'

'Sometimes, Watson,' he said, wearily, 'I despair of you. You have grasped sufficient of my methods to realise that I regard footprints at the scene of a crime as important, yet you have completely ignored the evidence of Constable Russell.'

'But Constable Russell said nothing of footprints!' I expostulated. 'And you made no enquiry on that point. I took particular note of it.'

'You would have done better to take particular note of the account given by Russell and to have understood what it meant.'

'I do not follow you,' I said, somewhat stiffly I admit.

'Constable Russell told us how he and most of the village were in the latter stages of the Harvest Feast when Mrs Collins arrived with the probationer constable and the search began. It was well after dark and the search parties were armed with torches. At around midnight, a party led by the farmer Grainger discovered the little girl's body. Russell's party and the others then assembled at the spot. Is that not sufficient?'

I was still puzzled and said so.

'By torchlight, Watson, a large body of men, most if not all of whom have taken drink, assemble at the Mayfield around the corpse of poor Bea Collins. Can you imagine for one moment that daylight will have revealed any traces around that spot apart from the myriad impressions of agricultural boots?'

'No,' I admitted, 'I suppose not.'

'Very well, Watson. If you have quite done requiring me to restate the obvious, perhaps you will be good enough to amuse yourself with your book.'

I saw that I had trespassed upon his patience far enough and, for the remainder of our journey, applied myself to the volume of sea stories that I had brought along.

Eventually we changed trains from the main line and came to Weston Stacey by a branch line of many stops and halts. The station was a little distant from the village, but a trap stood in the yard and its driver readily agreed to carry us to the John Barleycorn. As we rattled along the sunken lane to the village I looked around at the green hedgerows, behind which a slight breeze was rippling the ripening corn in the fields. My holiday mood returned.

'By Jove!' I exclaimed to Holmes. 'I had far rather be here in August than in Baker Street!'

He turned an expressionless face to me. 'I would remind you, Watson, that in one of these sunlit fields an innocent child was brutally killed and that her killer is still at large.'

Despite the warm afternoon his words chilled me.

6

JOHN BARLEYCORN

'Might I bring you another bottle from the cellar, gentlemen?' asked the landlord of the John Barleycorn as Holmes and I sat in the private back parlour.

We had finished an excellent dinner and were enjoying our pipes. 'No, thank you. I think not,' said Holmes. 'I rather fancy sampling some of your admirable local cider.'

'I shall bring you a jug at once,' said our host, but Holmes lifted a hand to stop him.

'Do not trouble yourself, landlord. My friend and I will take a glass in your public bar. At the same time we shall be able to make the acquaintance of some of your customers and perhaps I may pursue my researches.'

Holmes had passed us off to the innkeeper as holidaymakers, I a writer for magazines and he an amateur of folklore who had come to pass a few summer days in the village.

'Very well, gentlemen,' said the landlord, 'but do mind the cider. Some as is not used to it finds it outway strong.'

We made our way to the principal bar of the house, a great L-shaped room that occupied all the front of the ground floor and one side.

Holmes selected a table in the junction of the L, from where we could observe the entire room, and sent the potboy for two glasses of cider.

It was early evening and there were yet only a few drinkers, some sitting at tables and one or two standing at the bar. The leaded windows were thrown wide to admit a little air, and the lowering evening sun slanted through into the dark low-ceilinged room, lighting the red quarry tiles that made the floor and sparkling on the quaint horse brasses that hung here and there. Above our heads the ceiling was supported upon great beams of oak, black with age and generations of fires in the wide fireplace that now held only a basket of unlit logs. I could not help feeling that we were in the heart of an England that was almost unknown to dwellers in our great cities, an England at once more robust and kindlier than the frenzied world of London.

I took a long pull at my cider, a bright, clear yellow liquid with a clean strong flavour. 'Upon my word, Holmes!' I exclaimed. 'At times like this I wonder that I do not set up my practice in some village such as this and leave London and its fog and its crime and its dirt to you.'

He smiled, thinly. 'There are,' he said, 'fewer people dwelling in this village than occupy Baker Street, yet we are here to enquire into the brutal killing of a defenceless little girl. When do you recall such an event taking place on Baker Street? You do not— because it would not happen where so many people might see it done. I have observed before, Watson, that the countryside produces a strong sentiment in you; you see old inns and pretty cottages, smiling fields and handsome mansions—I see woods and waste places, marshes and pools, lonely houses far from the observation of a neighbour, where the darkest crimes may be committed with impunity.'

I had known Sherlock Holmes for upwards of twenty years and I should have recalled that his response to the countryside was definitely not mine. His remarks had once again completely banished my mood and I sought to change the subject. 'Look,' I said, indicating a number of objects which hung from the beams above us. 'Those are the corn dollies to which Constable Russell referred.'

He stood up and stepped across to examine them. They were roughly cigar-shaped and between ten and twelve inches long. Each was constructed of stalks of corn bent and plaited into an elaborate spiral pattern, with decorative tufts at the ends.

'Some of them,' he remarked as he sat down again, 'have hung so long they are as black as the beams. What is their purpose?'

'I don't know that they have any genuine purpose,' I said. 'The children make them, mostly the girls, and they hang in houses from one harvest to another. I suppose that they are a charm to bring a good harvest in the following year.'

He nodded. 'It brought no good fortune to little Bea Collins,' he said.

For some time we drank and chatted on a variety of topics while the bar slowly filled with villagers but I noted that my friend's eyes were never still. Each new arrival was closely scrutinised by those wonderful eyes and I had no doubt that Holmes' astonishing ability to deduce information about a man without a word was being applied to all of them.

It was growing late in the evening and with the windows now closed against the night chill the inn's bar had developed that smoky atmosphere which so delighted Holmes at Baker Street. Away to our left a group of men had started taking it in turns to sing songs, supported by their fellows in the refrains. It was decorously done, one of the number acting as chairman of the proceedings, rapping the table with a cribbage board, announcing each performer and calling for order. I heard a number of songs that I had not heard since my boyhood in Hampshire, both lusty drinking songs like 'The Punch Ladle' and sweeter airs like 'The Lark In The Morning.'

The singing had drawn me back into my earlier mood when the door of the inn opened to reveal our friend Constable Russell. We had agreed that our previous contact should remain secret and we no more acknowledged him than he did us. He was in uniform and behind him came an impressive figure of a man also in police uniform. This could only be Sergeant Bullington. He was more than six feet tall and bore himself well, though he was running to fat. His uniform was immaculate and he carried in his hand a long stick, topped with a silver knob.

Followed by Russell the sergeant went to the bar and spoke a few words to the landlord, then began a stately progress around the big room, greeting persons at each table by name and being greeted, though I noted more than one face that lost its smile as soon as the sergeant's broad back was turned.

He came last to our corner, standing beside the table with PC Russell a pace behind him.

'Good evening, gentlemen,' he said. 'The landlord tells me you are taking a holiday in our village.'

'We are indeed,' said Holmes, 'though I think that is not against the law,' and he smiled broadly.

'No, sir. Not at all,' said the sergeant, 'but you will allow that it is my affair to know what is going forward in the village. Might I ask what brings you here? We are a bit out of the way.'

'Of course it is your affair, Sergeant, and I meant no harm by my pleasantry,' smiled Holmes. 'My friend is simply a writer for

London magazines, who felt the need of a little country air in this fine summer, whereas I am fortunate enough to be a man of leisure, able to pursue an interest in folklore. It is principally that which brings us here as the harvest approaches. I have been told that some picturesque customs are still practised hereabouts at harvest time and had hoped to witness them.'

'Folklore,' said the sergeant. 'I'm not sure that I take your meaning, sir.'

Holmes waved a hand expansively at an empty chair. 'If we might offer you refreshment, I shall be happy to explain,' he said.

The sergeant, tightly buttoned into a thick serge uniform, the stiff collar of which was cutting into his fleshy neck, looked thoughtfully at our mugs of cider. 'It would not be proper for me to accept your kind offer while on duty, sir, but then . . .' He paused and drew a large watch from beneath his tunic, glanced at it and thrust it back. 'It seems my duty time ended some minutes gone. Constable Russell, do you get off to the station and look after affairs there. I shall be along to sign the duty over to you when the Barleycorn closes.'

Russell saluted smartly and left the inn, still with no acknowledgement of us. Sergeant Bullington removed his helmet and laid it carefully on an empty seat along with his silver-mounted stick, then lowered himself into another chair. Holmes waved a hand for the potboy, who came to take the sergeant's order for a pint of pale ale and to renew our cider.

'Were you long in India?' asked my friend, once the drinks were supplied.

The police officer stared at him. 'Now how did you know that?' he said.

'I took you to be a former military man from your bearing,' said Holmes, 'and though I caught only a glimpse of your watch it confirmed my impression inasmuch as the case bears an inscription to Sergeant-Major Bullington. I dare say that your duties in the open air in weather such as we are experiencing impart a degree of colour to your face, but your tan is more deep-laid than any English sun imparts. Finally, your chosen drink is pale ale. Now the Midlands drinks mild ale and the West Country drinks cider or bitter, but pale ale was first brewed for the Army in India and remains the choice of many who acquired the taste there.'

'Why,' exclaimed the sergeant, 'you are better than a fortune-teller, sir. That was quite remarkable.'

'Oh, I can tell you nothing of your future,' said my friend. 'I claim no psychic powers but merely exercise a habit of observation and deduction in which I have trained myself. I can, however, hazard an opinion that, on leaving the Army, you joined the police, not in this county, but in a city force, possibly

Liverpool.'

'Wonderful!' said the sergeant. 'I was sergeant-major with the Royal West Mallows in India for a good few years, and happy to have stayed a good few more. The country suited me, as it does not suit some, but I was mustered out and landed on the dockside at Liverpool with neither family nor friends in this country and no occupation.'

I recalled my own return from India and my arrival at Portsmouth, a man without family, friends, health or occupation.

'I sympathise,' I said. 'Some twenty years ago I found myself in similar circumstances, home from the Afghan campaign with nothing to show for it but ruined health and the scars of a couple of jezail bullets.'

He lifted his glass to me. 'I saw a fair few skirmishes,' he said, 'but never a ball came near me. Tell me, sir,' he said turning to Holmes, 'how you knew I joined the force in Liverpool?'

'I did not say I knew,' Holmes corrected him. 'I said that I would hazard such an opinion. My reasons were twofold—firstly, your accent which is from well north of here and secondly your handsome staff. I do not claim an acquaintance with the police of every town and county, but I have observed senior sergeants carrying such a staff in Liverpool. Indeed, I have seen a head or two broken in the Flying Dutchman and the American Bar.'

The sergeant laughed. 'You are quite right,' he said. 'I was born in Cheshire, but was so long in India that I had no home to return to. There were men wanted for the Liverpool force when I came home and so I took up a new occupation. I earned my stripes in Liverpool and I can't say I didn't enjoy it, but with the years mounting up I lost the taste for rough and tumbles in sailor pubs so I found myself a quieter place to end my service.'

He paused and drew a prodigious swallow of his ale.

'But you know the Flying Dutchman and the American Bar, sir,' he went on. 'What would take a gentleman like yourself into such places?'

For a moment I thought that Holmes had overreached himself and given away his masquerade, but he was, as ever, equal to the occasion.

'I knew them well once,' he said, 'as I knew every sailor's tavern I could find. I was about to explain my hobby to you, Sergeant—the study of folklore. As others collect postage stamps or geological specimens, I collect the songs, stories and customs of the labouring people. I like to think of them as fragments from a simpler time, before machines took over everything.'

He gazed at the sergeant with an expression of such simple enthusiasm I could have laughed aloud.

'I see,' said the police officer. 'Well, there are customs here, as you've mentioned, and songs as you will have heard.'

'Oh yes,' said Holmes, spiritedly. 'We were listening to the singing before you came in.'

As though on cue the chairman of the group that had been singing rapped his cribbage board against the table. 'Order, gentlemen!' he cried. 'Mr Charlie Coomber is standing. Best of good order, please!'

A man in middle age, dressed like his fellow labourers and with his face burned red by the sun, had risen and was standing.

A voice called out, 'Give us "John Barleycorn", Charlie!'

The performer nodded and, without further ado, launched into his song. It was not one that I had heard before, though the melody seemed to be akin to that of the old convict ballad 'Van Diemen's Land.' What struck me forcibly, as the song went on, was the strange story that it told. I scribbled a few notes of it in my pocketbook at the time, and with the assistance of my friend's astonishing memory I was able to write all of the song out later that night. I reproduce it here with the exception of one vulgarity:

There were three men came out of the West,
  their fortune for to try,
And these three men swore a solemn oath
  John Barleycorn should die,

One of them said to drown him deep and
    another to hang him high,
For whoever follows the barley grain, a-
    begging will he die.

They ploughed him into the earth so deep, and
    the drags ran over his head,
And these three men swore a solemn oath
    John Barleycorn was dead,
There he lay in the cold, cold ground, till the
    rain from the sky did fall,
And John Barleycorn sprang up again and
    made liars of them all.

And there he stood till Midsummer came,
    a-looking all pale and wan,
Then John Barleycorn grew a long, long
    beard, and so became a man.
They hired men with scythes so sharp, who
    used him barbarously,
They caught him by his middle so small and
    cut him off at the knee.

Then next there came the binder who looked
    on him with a frown,
But John Barleycorn held a thistle stalk that
    pulled his courage down,
The farmer came with his pitchfork and he
    pierced him to the heart,
Like a thief, a rogue or a highwayman they
    tied him to a cart.

And then they brought him to a barn, a
  prisoner to endure,
But soon they fetched him out again and laid
  him on the floor,
They brought the threshers with their crabtree
  sticks to beat him flesh and bone,
But the miller he served him worse than that,
  for he ground him between two stones.

They flung him into a cistern deep and
  drowned him in water clear,
But the brewer he served him worse than that,
  for he brewed him into beer,
They used him in the kitchen then and they
  used him in the hall,
And they used him in the parlour there,
  among the ladies all.

Oh John Barleycorn is the finest man that ever
  grew in the land,
He will warm your heart and fetch a smile by
  the turning of your hand,
He will turn a boy into a man and a man into
  an ass,
He will change your gold into silver and your
  silver into brass.

John Barleycorn has a very great strength that
  will make men sigh and moan,
For the grip of his hand will make a man
  forget his wife and home,
But the drunkard is a wicked man who used

him worst of all,
For he took him up all in his mouth and
****** him against a wall.

John Barleycorn will make them hunt as never
wound a horn,
He will bring the tinker to the stocks, that
people may him scorn,
Put your red wine in a bottle and your cider in
a can,
John Barleycorn in a little brown bowl will
prove the stronger man.

Absolute silence reigned in the inn while Coomber sang his strange and savage ballad and there was no applause at the end, only a few cries of appreciation from his fellows.

Holmes, still in his character as the amateur of folklore, was staring at the singer with rapt attention. 'Wonderful!' he exclaimed as the song ended. 'A native song that characterises the spirit of the corn—a direct link to the beliefs of the ancients. You see now, Sergeant, what I meant when I said that the beliefs of a past age still survive in the memories of the unlettered labourer. I doubt if Coomber there can write his own name, but he carries that marvellous song that expresses a belief older by far than Christianity.'

The sergeant did not appear to share my friend's enthusiasm. 'I dare say you're right, sir,' he said. 'There are a number of things the farm labourers hereabouts believe that seem a bit strange and old-fashioned though I think they're just superstitions and that. Still, gentlemen, if you're proposing to enquire into them, I recommend that you go a bit careful. Some of the people hereabouts set a lot of store by their old beliefs and they might not like gentlemen like yourself asking about them.'

'Oh, I quite understand,' said Holmes. 'We shall be entirely discreet in our approaches, I assure you.'

The sergeant rose and picked up his helmet and staff. 'I thank you for your hospitality, gentlemen,' he said. 'If I can be of service to you while you are here, you know where to find me.'

We thanked him and bade him goodnight, then made our way to our rooms.

7

THE MAYFIELD

Whether it was the country air, our long journey from London or the cider which I had consumed, I slept deeply that night and rose rather later than usual next morning. I was surprised on entering the inn's back parlour not to see Holmes already at the table, but our landlord informed me that my friend had left the premises early, leaving word that he would rejoin me in time for breakfast.

Sherlock Holmes has never been convinced of the virtues of fresh air, nor of the concept of physical activity for its own sake, and I was certain that he had not merely taken a morning walk. His absence, I knew, betokened some development in his plans, and I drank tea impatiently while I awaited his return.

I did not have long to wait before he strode in. He had become the complete holidaymaker, in linen suit and straw hat, and carried a stout ash stick. I knew the stick to contain a concealed blade, for I had seen it flash gold in the firelight when he first wielded it on a Welsh hillside some years earlier [See *Sherlock Holmes and the Devil's Grail*, Constable, 1996.], and I hoped that he had not gone about some risky enterprise without me.

He dropped his hat and stick on a chair and came to the table where he poured himself a cup of tea and lifted the bell to ring for the landlord.

'You went out armed, I see,' I said, nodding towards his stick.

'Purely a precaution,' he said. 'You need not fear that I have been putting myself in danger without your sturdy presence. I have merely been collecting further data.'

'Really?' I said. 'Of what kind?'

'Knowing that our friend PC Russell was on

duty during the night, I thought it best to waylay him out of his sergeant's company and ask him what one usually asks a policeman,' said Holmes.

'The time!' I exclaimed. 'But, Holmes—'

'No, Watson,' he interrupted. 'I simply asked our friend the way to Buckstone and how to find the Mayfield.'

I was disappointed. 'Then we are going to view the scene of the crime?' I asked. 'Surely it will tell even you very little after a year?'

'It told the county police nothing at the time. I had much rather have seen it a year ago and without the intrusion of drunken labourers' boots when it might have revealed much to me. Nevertheless, it may still have some little indication for me.'

The landlord arrived and we busied ourselves with breakfast. Once we had eaten, Holmes must be off at once, about what I confess I considered to be a pointless exercise. Despite the sunny morning and the pleasant landscape of small copses and fields of ripening corn through which we strolled, I remained convinced that we were wasting our time. I freely admit, with the benefit of hindsight, that three matters came to our notice as a result of that morning's stroll that were instrumental in unravelling one of the darkest cases which my friend ever investigated.

We found the Mayfield easily with

Constable Russell's directions. It lay, as he had said, almost midway between the village and the hamlet of Buckstone, a large field, rising from its four sides to a slight eminence at the centre. It was thick with corn that stood high and was turning from green to ripe gold, but a well-worn footpath ran from a corner adjacent to the road, across the field's centre to a diagonally opposite corner.

We climbed the stile that led into the Mayfield and walked between the high rows of corn. Holmes had fallen silent and his keen eyes were fixed on the dry, beaten earth that formed the path. Once or twice he paused and probed with his stick at the soil or at the roots of the corn.

Our path was not straight, but curved a little near to the top of the rise and, as we rounded that curve, we came across a tableau that would have made a pretty and affecting painting for one of our great illustrators. The sad little sunlit scene remains fresh in my memory after two decades.

Between the walls of corn knelt a little girl of about eleven years. Her boots were broken and dusty and her clothing clean but badly worn and she was evidently a local labourer's child. Her head was bare and tears sparkled on her sun-browned cheeks as she knelt silently in the shade of the tall grain stalks. In front of her, set just within the wall of cornstalks, stood a pile of rough stones and on that stone lay a fresh bunch of wild flowers, tied with a strand of blue ribbon.

It was evident that we had come upon this pretty child as she knelt in sorrow before some little local shrine. At our approach she looked up, startled, and commenced to rise, but Sherlock Holmes lifted a hand.

'No, my dear,' he said, in his kindliest tones. 'We have no wish to disturb you. If we had seen you we would not have interrupted, but the corn hid you. Were you praying for Bea Collins?'

As scathingly sarcastic as my friend could be, when dealing with children he was the soul of kindness and seemed to bear an almost hypnotic ability to elicit a trusting response from them. Our little stranger choked down a sob and nodded to his question.

'And do the stones mark where she was found?' he asked.

The child found her voice. 'That's right, sir,' she said. 'This is where they found her. We all put a stone here so she should not be forgotten. Some on us brings flowers for her.'

'She was a friend of yours?' asked Holmes.

'Yes, sir,' said the little girl. 'She was my best friend. We was at school together and she lived in the same row and we even worked together in the fields but now she's gone,' and with the last word her tears broke afresh and she wept openly.

Holmes squatted and touched the child's

shaking shoulder and I hunkered down beside him.

'She has gone to a better world,' I said, for her sorrow for her friend had touched me deeply.

'I know,' she sobbed. 'Mr Trentham, that's the parson, sir, he said as Bea's gone where no one can do her no more harm, but she'll be alone.'

It is a doctor's duty to bring comfort where he can and I tried again. 'One day,' I said, 'you shall be with her and it will be as though you were never apart. I promise you.'

She rubbed her streaming eyes. 'I do hope so, sir. I really do.'

'What is your name?' asked Holmes.

'Alice,' she said, 'Alice Moyce, please, sir.'

'Well, Alice,' said Holmes, and his hand was still on her shoulder, 'my friend and I would very much like to hear what you may know about how Bea Collins came to her death.'

She looked puzzled. 'Nobody knows, sir,' she said. 'She was just coming home from the harvest last Feast Day and she never got home. The grown-ups all went looking for her when she never come home and they found her here and something had killed her. Even Sergeant Bullington don't know what happened.'

'And has no one said anything to you, have you heard nobody say anything about how poor little Bea was killed?' he asked.

She shook her head. 'No, sir. That is, apart

from Billy Hayter.'

'And what did Billy Hayter say?'

'Billy Hayter says as there's a thing in the woods that kills children. He says he seen it once by the Buckstone and it was all painted and had skulls.'

'Skulls!' I ejaculated. 'Did he say "skulls"?'

'Yes, sir,' she said. 'I didn't know what he meant, I mean things only has one skull, but Billy said as this thing had lots of them.'

Holmes looked at me across the child's head in frank puzzlement. 'Who is Billy Hayter?' he asked.

'He's a big boy,' she said. 'He lives in Buckstone.'

'And would he be at home now?' asked Holmes.

She shook her head again. 'Oh no, sir. He's away with his father at the harvesting. He won't be back again until the harvest starts here.'

Holmes straightened up and felt in his pocket for a coin. 'I'm sorry we disturbed you,' he said, 'but we are pleased to have met you. We are staying at the John Barleycorn and you will see us about. If you ever hear more about your friend's death, you tell us, will you, Alice?'

He pressed the coin into her little brown hand and she looked at it wide-eyed. 'Oh thank you, sir. Yes, sir. I'll tell you anything I hear.'

She skipped away, her sorrow evaporated, but after only a few steps she turned back.

'I did hear one thing else,' she said. 'I heard Mr Platt, the harvest master. He said as we should be careful, all us little ones, and not dawdle or play about on the way to or from the fields. He told us always to stay in twos or threes and not go alone on the road in the morning nor the evening.'

'And was this after Bea's death?' asked Holmes.

'That's right,' she said. 'He got us all together and said that we must be very careful and stay together.'

'Did he say why?' asked my friend.

'No, sir. He only said as there was bad people about that might do us harm.'

Holmes thanked her again and she skipped away, towards the Buckstone road. He looked after her for a moment with a thoughtful expression, then turned his attention back to the ground.

I have learned over the years to stand well aside when Sherlock Holmes sets out to examine an area, such is the enthusiasm with which he falls to his task, and this unpromising site was no exception. As soon as our little friend was out of sight he was on his knees on the path touching and fingering the soil, peering between the stalks of corn, lifting the stones at the edges of the little cairn and probing between them with his fingers. After several minutes of this he whipped his magnifying lens from his pocket and began to move it across the path, peering intently through it.

I realised that he was observing a column of ants which was moving along one of the tiny tracks they create, from the edge of the little memorial cairn to the opposite side of the footpath, where they were disappearing into and emerging from a small hole.

'Salt!' he exclaimed after a few seconds, then, 'No! Sugar!'

I watched in puzzlement, having not the least idea what information he might derive from the ants. Holmes followed their path back to the pile of stones and lifted the stone alongside the spot where they were entering the cairn. From behind it he lifted something, glanced at it briefly and slipped it into his pocket before continuing his examination of the ground. I am well aware that my powers of observation are greatly inferior to those of my friend and I merely awaited his explanation of his findings.

At last he stood up, picked up his stick and brushed down the knees of his trousers.

'You are wrong, Watson,' he said.

'I beg your pardon, Holmes . . .' I began but he silenced me with a raised hand.

'You were thinking,' he said, 'that the death of Bea Collins was so similar to that of Fanny Adams, with which you are no doubt familiar, that the cause must be the same.'

'Great heavens Holmes!' I exclaimed. 'I know you always explain these things and they seem very simple, but even now it still disturbs me when you read my mind so accurately.'

He shook his head ruefully. 'After so many years you still refer to my endeavours as mind-reading,' he said. 'You know very well that it is more a case of reading movements, facial expressions, gestures and so on in order to deduce what the mind is thinking. In this case you looked at the little pile of stones and you looked around at the field. Then you began to hum quietly, an air which I am sure I recognised as the old song of "Sweet Fanny Adams". You were thinking that there is a field in Hampshire where a similar cairn marks the spot where Fanny Adams met her fate and it reminded you of the view you expressed in London, that Bea Collins, like Fanny Adams, was the victim of a lunatic. I have explained to you why you are in error.'

'You are quite right,' I conceded, 'but it still seems like witchcraft to me.'

'Witchcraft?' repeated a strange voice. 'Now there's a peculiar subject for two gentlemen to be discussing in a field of corn on a fine summer's morning.'

We turned to find that, as we had surprised little Alice Moyce, we had been surprised by a tall, elderly man in clerical grey. Under his wide-brimmed straw hat a long, keen face was lit by two bright blue eyes.

'Let me introduce myself,' he said. 'I am Theodore Trentham, the incumbent of Weston Stacey. I believe that you must be the two holidaymakers who are lodged at the John Barleycorn.'

Holmes confirmed the vicar's guess and introduced us under the pseudonyms we had adopted. 'You need not be surprised at our discussion of witchcraft,' he continued. 'I am an amateur of folklore and was moved to wonder at the purpose of this little cairn with its votive flowers. It occurred to me that it might have some superstitious significance and I was commenting to my friend on the strange survivals of paganism and witchcraft that are still to be found in our countryside, even in the twentieth century.'

The clergyman shook his head sadly. 'No, no,' he said. 'For once I wish it was one of those curious customs, but it is not. This is a memorial erected by the children of the area to the memory of one of their number who was cruelly murdered at this spot a year ago.'

Holmes expressed his astonishment and, thus encouraged, the vicar told us of Bea Collins' death, adding nothing that we did not know. When he had done we expressed our sorrow that such a charming spot should be visited by violence.

'I thank you, gentlemen,' he said. 'But let us turn to more cheerful things. My own niece is like you, sir, an amateur of folklore, and I feel sure she would wish to make your acquaintance. May I tell her of our meeting and would you, perhaps, join us for tea one afternoon?'

We expressed our willingness and the vicar lifted his hat to us and strode on his way. I could not resist chaffing Holmes. 'Well,' I said, 'our visit to the *locus in quo* has produced nothing except an invitation to take tea with the vicar.'

'Not so, Watson, not so,' he said. 'It has produced the story of the painted thing with skulls which Billy Hayter saw . . .'

'A boy's fantasy to frighten little girls,' I said. 'Surely you do not take that seriously?'

'We shall see, in due time, how seriously Master Hayter takes it. Then, perhaps, we shall judge. We have also made a friend of Alice, who will act as our eyes and ears among the community's children, where we could not go. We have discovered that Mr Platt, the harvest master, expressed concern for the safety of his little gangers—an unlikely action for such a man. We have made ourselves welcome at the vicarage, where we may gather more data, if not about the crime, at least about the parish and its congregation, and finally—we have discovered this.'

He drew from his pocket the object which he had extracted from among the stones, and I saw that it was a fragment of paper. I took it from him and examined it. It was coarse paper, torn at the edges, faintly blue in colour but faded by weather. Something whitish and crystalline clung to a fold. I prodded at it with my finger.

'It is sugar,' said Holmes. 'It has been moistened and hardened again. That was what attracted the ants. They were carrying tiny fragments of sugar to their nest.'

'It is certainly a fragment of sugar-paper,' I said. 'But I imagine it has been dropped by some child visiting the cairn. They will have had sweets in it.'

He shook his head. 'Sweets,' he said, 'are usually served in twists of plain white paper. Only sugar is served in that thick blue.'

'But why do you associate it with the crime?' I asked, mystified. 'It may have been dropped by anyone at any time.'

'True,' he said. 'At this stage I cannot definitely associate this fragment with the death of the child. I hope that you are right, Watson, for if you are not, then we may be dealing with something that belongs in nightmares, not in an English cornfield.'

I looked at the tattered scrap in my hand and from it to my friend's face. I saw that, whatever the meaning of his dark foreboding, he was completely serious.

8

THE PLACE OF BONES

The huge key grated in the ancient lock and the door creaked on its iron hinges, swinging slowly open to release a smell of dust and earth. From the hot, sunny afternoon Holmes and I stepped into the dark, chilly chamber beyond the door.

True to his word, the Reverend Trentham had delivered a note to the inn on the morning after our chance meeting, inviting us to join him and his niece for afternoon tea and, if we wished, to come a little early and see the church.

Sherlock Holmes was not a sociable man. He never visited friends nor invited them to dine. Indeed, more than once he had done me the honour of stating that I was his only friend. Although I knew him to be ever courteous to the fair sex, it crossed my mind that he might manifest the more impatient side of his nature if the Reverend Trentham bored us with his tour of the church, and I was a little nervous as we set out.

Our landlord had told us that a footpath at the back of the inn would take us across a meadow to the rear gate of the churchyard, and, as we climbed the stile into the cemetery, we saw our host waiting at the church's main door. He welcomed us effusively and gave us a brief history of his building. It had been an Anglo-Saxon foundation, the original charter dating from 765, and Holmes delighted the vicar by telling him that he had seen the original document in the Diocesan records at Salisbury. I had forgotten Holmes' hobby of delving into early charters and was pleased to see this cordial beginning. While I strolled behind, the clergyman took us through his church, pointing out the Norman alterations, the curious stained glass lozenges in two windows depicting the characters of a mummers' play, and the heraldry and symbolism in other windows, whilst intermittently disputing with Holmes whether Augustine had brought Christianity to Britain or whether he had imposed the rule of the Roman Church on an island which had been substantially converted long before.

We had completed the tour, as we believed, and returned to the main door when the vicar took a large key from his pocket and led us along a little-used footpath at the side of the building. We came to a short flight of worn stone steps, leading down to a large door, set into the lower level of the church. Opening the door, our guide stepped aside and invited us to enter.

The chamber into which Holmes and I

stepped was lit only by sunlight falling from the open door. Beyond that it stretched away into darkness and seemed, so far as one could see, to penetrate some distance under the church's main building. As we stood in the little patch of daylight we were surrounded by skulls and bones, piled high on rows of shelves which lined both side walls.

'Good heavens, Holmes!' I exclaimed. 'A charnel house!'

'More correctly,' he reproved me, 'an ossuary.'

'Indeed,' said the vicar, from behind us. 'There are few such remaining in England.'

'But what is its purpose?' I asked.

'Until fairly recent times,' said the vicar, 'it was the custom to bury the dead wrapped only in woollen cloth and uncoffined. When new burials occurred, the grave-diggers would disturb the remains of former interments and, to accommodate the new burial, the old bones would be taken from the ground and placed here, so as to remain on sanctified ground. It was a convenience which obviated extending the graveyard every few years.'

I looked around me and shuddered. Holmes, of course, had his lens in hand and was examining some of the nearer skulls with minute attention. It was obvious that the place had been in use for a very long time, for some of the skulls and bones that we could see were crumbled so that they were almost unrecognisable while others were seemingly solid and readily identifiable as human remains though all were covered in heavy dust.

The dissecting room and the demonstration skeleton teach medical students to be unaffected by the sight of human parts and remains, and I hold my nerve to be as steady as the next man's, but the sight of this charnel display, come upon unexpectedly on a bright August afternoon, had, I admit, chilled me, and I could have wished that Holmes would pay less attention to the grisly collection and let us be about our tea.

At length my friend straightened himself and pocketed his lens. 'They are remarkable,' he assured the vicar. 'I hope that good care is taken to protect them.'

The Reverend Trentham chuckled. 'As to that,' he said, 'none of our village hooligans— and sadly there are some—would set foot inside this door. If they wished to it would be easy, for the key hangs in the church, but their superstition keeps them well clear of the graveyard at night. Even at this time of year, when the evenings are bright, the choirboys run from the church after practice, lest twilight find them in the churchyard. No—those relics will remain safe here until Judgement Day.'

We returned to the outer world and our host locked the ancient door behind us. When he had returned the key to the vestry, we followed him across the churchyard to the vicarage while he explained that the mound on which the church stood was believed to have been a pagan burial place, adapted to Christian purposes in accordance with the direction of Pope Gregory that such spots should be the site of Christian worship.

A uniformed maid took our hats and sticks at the vicarage door and informed us that Miss Thorne had ordered tea to be laid in the garden as the day was so warm. Behind the house, a flight of steps from a wide terrace led on to a spacious lawn with flower-beds on each flank. At the foot of the lawn a great wide cedar tree spread its shade, beneath which we could see our hostess awaiting us.

She rose from the table as her uncle introduced us under our assumed names, a tall woman of some thirty years, pleasingly slender and with wide, dark eyes in an attractive face. Beneath her summer hat those eyes seemed to glitter with amusement as her uncle made the introductions and I was a little puzzled until she spoke.

'I do not know, Uncle Teddy,' she said with a little chuckle, 'whether you have made one of your little mistakes, or whether these gentlemen have been pulling your leg, but I can assure you that they are not the people you believe them to be. Do you not recognise the celebrated consulting detective, Mr Sherlock Holmes, and his equally celebrated amanuensis, Dr Watson?'

There was a moment's silence, while the Reverend Trentham looked confused and I looked to Holmes for a reaction. Then my friend took Miss Thorne's extended hand and bowed over it.

'You are singularly perceptive, Miss Thorne,' he said.

'Not at all, Mr Holmes,' she said, as we took our places around the table. 'Ever since my return to England I have been following Dr Watson's accounts of your exploits in the *Strand*. It would be difficult not to recognise you both from Mr Paget's excellent representations of you.'

Her uncle, plainly bewildered, protested. 'But Cecily—' but she cut him off with another chuckle.

'Do not worry, Uncle. I have no doubt that Mr Holmes and the Doctor have good reason for posing as a pair of holidaying amateurs of folklore. I am honoured to make their acquaintance, though I had looked forward to a discussion on aspects of folklore.'

'We apologise,' said Holmes, 'for our small deception, but you will, I am sure, realise that in a community as small as Weston Stacey it would not do to have everyone knowing that Sherlock Holmes was at large. I have found that this knowledge can produce an unhealthy disturbance among wrongdoers and confuse my enquiries. As to folklore, Miss Thorne, it is a necessary part of the studies of a criminal

73

agent. Superstition plays a considerable part in detection.'

'In what way, Mr, er, Holmes?' enquired the vicar.

'Why,' said Holmes, 'a man's superstitions are as much a part of him as his language. He acquires them at his mother's knee. If a man balks at a black cat, he is American—if he welcomes it as a good omen, he is British, or of British descent. A man who cannot bear the mention of rabbits will be from the so-called "island" of Portland in Dorset. Superstition may even be the cause of crime. There are murders in the furtherance of superstitious belief, thefts of ritual objects which have no value except to a believer, executions of those who have betrayed their fellow believers. I cannot pretend that folklore is my special study, Miss Thorne, but I own to a deep professional interest in the subject.'

Our hostess smiled. 'Then we shall not tax you with the reasons why you and Dr Watson are in Weston Stacey under assumed names, Mr Holmes, but keep our conversation on the intended lines. No doubt my uncle has shown you the remarkable stained glass in the church with the mumming figures. Are they not very attractive and extremely quaint?'

'They are,' said Holmes, 'both quaint and attractive, and it is rare, I believe, to find a pagan observance celebrated in stained glass in a Christian building.'

'That is true,' said the vicar, nodding. 'Though there are other examples known. By and large, as I said on the way here, the Church applied Pope Gregory's directive that sites of pagan worship should be taken over, as it were, if the people could not be persuaded to turn away from them, but many churches and cathedrals bear evidence of pagan masons inserting figures from their pantheon among the decorated stonework, some of them, alas, of an indecent nature. By the time stained glass became possible, most of those beliefs had died away or dwindled into insignificance, I am glad to say.'

'Oh, Uncle Teddy!' chided his niece. 'You yourself have said that the best of paganism was an incomplete and uncomprehending attempt to find the true God and that we should not scorn man's early efforts to better himself. You cannot describe as indecent a mere celebration of the body.'

Her uncle blushed. 'What will our visitors think of you, Cecily! We are made in the image of our Maker, and it behoves us to use our bodies for his purposes alone. You are not unaware of my struggle to stamp out certain indelicate practices in connection with the sowing of crops because I deemed them to have little of worship and more of indecency in them, but when our village mummers call here in January I am happy to see their little play, for in essence the battle of St George and

Turkey Snipe is the battle of good and evil and the play serves to remind us of that eternal conflict and of the ultimate triumph of good.'

'For which reason,' said Holmes, 'it is among the oldest dramas in the world. I am sure that you will have seen similar plays enacted by strolling companies of village people while you were in India, Miss Thorne.'

'Now how did you know that I have been in India, Mr Holmes? Has my uncle been boring you with our family history?'

'Not at all,' said my friend. 'You yourself mentioned that you had been out of England. On this hot day you protect yourself from the sun of England beneath this handsome cedar, but there is a depth to your complexion that speaks of a hotter sun. Finally, the silver brooch which you wear is, if I am not mistaken, of Benares design and workmanship. I would go so far as to suggest that it is of sentimental significance to you, as it is too heavy for the material of your summer dress and pulls a little. You would not wear it with a light dress unless it meant more to you than mere decoration.'

She clapped her hands with delight. 'Oh, that was marvellous, Mr Holmes! You really are as good as Dr Watson has always said.'

'Extraordinary!' exclaimed the Reverend Trentham. 'In another day they would have burned you at the stake, Mr Holmes.'

My friend nodded in acknowledgement of

their applause.

'It is true,' continued the vicar, 'that my niece was many years in India. Her mother—my sister—was married to a fine Christian man who pursued a missionary calling. My late wife and I brought up their only child, Cecily here, until she was old enough to be sent out to join her parents in their work. When they were taken, she returned to the only home in this country which she has ever known,' and he gazed at her fondly.

She reached out for her uncle's hand and clasped it. 'My poor dear parents were victims of an epidemic in India,' she said, 'and I myself nearly succumbed. Had it not been for what some would scorn as superstition—the traditional healing practices of the native people—I would not have survived.'

My professional interest was aroused and I asked, 'May I ask what was the epidemic? Typhoid fever? Cholera morbus perhaps?'

She shook her head. 'It was a fierce fever, but one that seems peculiar to our location. Our mission's doctor and the military doctor in the cantonment were both unable to halt its spread. My own life was saved by what I believe was an intervention of the Almighty. My father had assisted a non-commissioned officer at the barracks who was in danger of losing his rank and place through his taste for spirits. Father showed that man that the satisfactions of religion are deeper and greater than the poisonous pleasures of the bottle and, when he heard of my parents' death and my own sickness, he brought a native woman to us, a healer among their people. She it was who plied me with her herbal mixtures and nursed me back to health.'

'Cast thy bread upon the waters . . .' murmured the vicar, glancing piously upward.

'Indeed,' responded Holmes. 'And the brooch?'

'Was a gift from my Mama,' said Cecily. 'I wear it always. You were exactly right, Mr Holmes.'

Recalling from a distance of nearly twenty years that sunny afternoon on the lawn of a country vicarage, makes it hard to believe that Holmes and I were really engaged in an investigation of something as dreadful as we ultimately discovered. The warm sun, the scent of flowers, the exchange of opinions across the tea-table, almost lulled me to the point of committing the unpardonable rudeness of falling asleep. I cannot now recollect all the exchanges between my three companions on the subject of folklore, superstition and religion. I know little of these things and was content to listen to the others.

At last the pleasant interlude ended. Our host and hostess led us through the vicarage to the front door. In the hall a scatter of large, red, white and blue posters lay on a table. Miss Thorne drew our attention to them.

'They are for the village's festivities at His Majesty's Coronation,' she explained. 'Uncle Teddy and I are on the committee. Will you still be with us then?'

'I imagine so,' said Holmes, 'but I would esteem it a favour if you would not reveal to anyone else our true identities.'

They both assured us that they would not do so, and we took our leave, Miss Thorne pressing a copy of the poster upon us as we left. In the days that followed I was to see copies of it often, nailed to trees, posted on the notice-board outside the Public Hall, in the church's porch and at a number of farm gates. I have my copy still, and I reproduce it at the end of this chapter, not merely as a curious reminder of a rural life which is already passing away with moving pictures and the gramophone, but because it was to play a strange part in the unravelling of the mystery that haunted Weston Stacey.

CORONATION OF KING EDWARD VII

Programme of

FESTIVITIES

to be held at Weston Stacey on

SATURDAY & MONDAY, AUGUST 9th & 11th

PROGRAMME – FIRST DAY – SATURDAY

10 O'CLOCK ROYAL SALUTE BY WELLSFORD FIRE BRIGADE

At 11 a.m. Services will be held in the Parish Church and Wesleyan
Chapel for Coronation and Thanksgiving for the King's Recovery

1.30 p.m. A PROCESSION

will be formed in the Cricket Field of all the Organisations in the Village
Prizes will be awarded for the Best Decorated Bicycles, Best Character on
Horseback or on Foot and Best Tradesman's Turnout

☞ THE COMMITTEE INVITE ALL TO ASSIST IN MAKING THIS A SUCCESS ☜

SPORTS will be held in the Cricket Field at 3.30 o'clock
by kind permission of Mr Henry Devaux

ALL ENTRIES FOR THE ORIGINAL DATE WILL STAND GOOD
also a display by Wellsford Fire Brigade

at 9 o'clock there will be a TORCHLIT PROCESSION

WHICH WILL PARADE THE VILLAGE -- FOLLOWED BY

A GRAND DISPLAY of FIREWORKS

A Prize of 2 Guineas will be given by Mr Geo. Devaux for the
BEST DECORATED FRONT with LIVE PLANTS
WELLSFORD SILVER BAND will be in attendance

PROGRAMME -- SECOND DAY -- MONDAY

Presentation of Medals to the Children at 12 noon in their schools

A PROCESSION AT ONE O'CLOCK

Children's Tea at 3:   Old People's Tea at 5:   In the Public Hall
✠ SPORTS ✠ ON ✠ THE ✠ CRICKET ✠ FIELD ✠
following the Children's Tea

AN ENTERTAINMENT in the Public Hall at 7 o'clock

with Performances by a Conjurer, Revd. Theodore Trentham at the
Pianoforte and a Presentation of Lantern Slides by Miss Cecily Thorne,
'CURIOSITIES of OUR INDIAN EMPIRE'

☜ **GOD SAVE THE KING** ☞

9

THE HARVEST LORD

We strolled back the way we had come, through the churchyard and across the meadow to the John Barleycorn, and I took the opportunity to ask if my friend had gleaned anything from our tea-time conversation.

'I have learned,' he said, thoughtfully, 'that Billy Hayter's strange tale may have some substance.'

'Heavens, Holmes!' I exclaimed. 'It is surely a fabrication by a malicious boy to frighten little girls.'

'You may yet prove right,' he said 'but I prefer to suspend judgement at least until I have had the opportunity of talking to Master Hayter.'

'I really do not see why you give it any credence at all,' I grumbled.

'Because,' he said, 'of coincidence. You know my view of coincidence, Watson, that it is the willing handmaiden of the lazy mind. As an explanation it explains nothing and frequently leads the enquirer away from the truth.'

'But what coincidence . . .' I began before the answer occurred to me. 'Oh! You mean the skulls?'

'Not just the skulls, Watson,' he said, 'but

81

the fact that Billy Hayter referred to "skulls" in the plural—a curious fact in itself since skulls usually come singly—and we have come across a quantity of skulls in this village, stored in an ossuary which is open to anyone who knows the whereabouts of the key, and some of which have certainly been removed, despite Mr Trentham's assertions.'

'Removed!' I exclaimed.

'I had thought that, for a scientific man, you displayed a certain unease in the ossuary,' he said. 'It seems to have affected your powers of observation. Firstly, there were footmarks plain in the thick dust on the floor, apparently the prints of a youth or a small man. Secondly, the bones, though of differing ages, had been placed on the shelves as they were found—that is, as complete or nearly-complete skeletons with their skulls. Some, indeed, had been loosely bound with string to keep them in a bundle. Yet there were, away from the door so that their absence would not be readily noticeable, a number of such bundles that had no skulls with them.'

'Perhaps the skulls were not found by the grave-diggers,' I hazarded.

'It is in the highest degree unlikely that there would be a sustained period during which all of the remains found in the churchyard lacked their skulls, Watson. It is evident that they have been removed from the ossuary. There is a further fact which may make the missing skulls significant.'

'What is that?' I asked.

'The abstracted skulls were all those of small children. So we have a murdered child, a tale of some strange creature with skulls and a quantity of children's skulls missing from the church, Watson.'

'What do you believe it all means?' I asked.

'I believe that they are all pieces of the same puzzle,' he said, 'but I refuse to theorise ahead of my data. Nevertheless, Watson, I am more certain than ever that we are dealing with something singularly evil.'

We followed our usual evening routine and, after dinner, took up our accustomed table in the bar. While we drank and chatted my friend's eyes and ears were ever alert for any small event or remark that he might add to his accumulation of data, but the little party of locals who shared the bar with us were intent upon games of backgammon.

Holmes was in a communicative mood, freely discoursing on the connection between the Romany tongue of the Gypsies and Hindustani, the traditional ballads of the lowland Scots and his belief that human blood contained substances that, if properly analysed, might identify the individual from whom the blood originated.

It was late on, nearly at the time when Sergeant Bullington would make his nightly round, when a newcomer entered the bar. He

83

was a man of middle height, with grizzled dark hair and a weathered, lean face. He wore a long tweed jacket over riding breeches and boots, a red neck-cloth and a brown high-crowned billycock hat. In his left hand he carried a small coiled whip.

The locals recognised him at once, greeting him with calls of 'Evening, Mr Platt,' and I heard one explain to another that this was the 'Harvest Lord.'

'This,' said Holmes to me, 'is a man I was very much hoping to meet.'

He had hardly spoken the words when the door opened again and Sergeant Bullington entered, accompanied by his probationer constable. Seeing Platt at the bar, the sergeant told off his constable to make the round of the room, while he made straight for the harvest master's side. Holmes watched, while the two stood at the bar and chatted for several minutes, then the sergeant summoned his probationer and left with an affable nod to us as he passed our table.

As soon as he was gone, Holmes went to the bar and engaged Platt in conversation. Very shortly they came to our table, carrying their drinks.

'This,' said Holmes, introducing the newcomer to me, 'is Mr Platt, who supplies the harvest labour around this village and will doubtless be able to tell us much of the customs that are connected with reaping.'

Platt sat and took a swallow of his drink. 'I don't know as I can be of much assistance, gentlemen,' he said, 'but I have been harvesting for a good many years now, from Dorset to the west and east as far as Berkshire.'

'I heard one of the local men call you the "Harvest Lord",' said Holmes. 'Is that your usual title?'

Platt laughed and shook his head. 'That's an old fashion,' he said. ' 'Tis just a word like they calls my best reaper my "Lady". Charlie Wells ain't no more of a Lady than he is a baboon and I ain't much of a Lord, am I, living from hand to mouth out of what's left from the contract fee once I've paid my gang? And for that I has to keep moving all summer long, from first haying to last corn.'

He took another drink then reached into an inside pocket of his coat, pulling out a folded paper and offering it across the table.

'There,' he said, 'is my terms. Same almost for every farm where I works.'

It was a printed sheet prepared, from its appearance, by some jobbing printer in the West Country. At this distance in time I do not recall all of its content, but I jotted a few of the principal points into my journal that night and I have them still. It read something like this:

HARVEST AGREEMENT with ALBERT PLATT
for .... FARM

The Company of Harvesters will be composed of 15 men (excepting men to handle horses) and shall do as follows:

1. Wheat cut by binder to be set up in rows across the field;
2. Wheat cut by reapers to be tied and set up in rows across the field;
3. All wheat to be carted and stacked in a workmanlike manner;
4. First lot of wheat rakings to be carted with sheaves if so required;
5. The Company to thresh for up to three days as required;
6. Machines to be driven by men of the Company;
7. All rakings to be gathered carted, stacked and drag-raked behind each cart;
8. Sheaves to be set up when fallen down as required;
9. Stacks to be covered each night and loads placed under cover;
10. Master to find drivers and leaders and do horse-raking;
11. Work to commence and finish according to Master's wishes;
12. If any harvestman be absent, remainder of Company shall do his

and their work and agree payment for same;

13 Each harvestman shall work so long as harvest shall last.

There were a number of other agreements and requirements, including a price to be paid to Platt for the services of his 'Company.' I recall that the last item read:

It is the option of the Master to give a Harvest Feast or not according to the behaviour and satisfaction given by the Company.

I returned the document to him. 'I had thought,' I said, 'that women and children also worked with your company.'

'So they do, sir,' he said. 'But they aren't paid by me. I shall bring in a few men, but more I shall hire roundabout, and they brings their womenfolk and little ones with them. That way, you see, they can get more work done. Besides, the women and children is better at binding the sheaves. The kiddies weaves the bond fast with their little fingers and the ladies is very expert at tying the sheaves.'

'I thought,' I said, 'that the law had regulated the employment of child labour in the harvest.'

'So it has,' he replied. 'First it was none

under eight years of age, then none under ten but no one pays it a mind. The parents sends any kiddies as can walk to the harvest and over in the east they're always short of harvestmen and they will take any children. Treats them very bad they do, too, some of the harvest masters in the east. I could make a lot more money if I was willing to work the east and go on the way they does, but I couldn't do it, gentlemen.'

Perhaps he saw scepticism in my face, for he went on, 'When there's little ones working with my gang I always tries to look out for them.' He tapped the whip that lay coiled on a chair beside him. 'That's for my old pony,' he said, 'and then only when he gets outway fractious. I ain't one of them harvest masters as walks the furrows behind the binders with my whip.'

'I am sure you are not,' said Holmes placatingly. 'In fact I have heard that after the death of little Bea Collins last year you took especial care to ensure that no other child came to harm.'

'Ah!' exclaimed Platt. 'Little Bea, what an awful thing that was, sir. Yes, I did warn them all not be alone and to look out for each other.'

'Did you have any idea of a particular danger?' asked Holmes.

Platt drew a long draught of his ale. ' 'Tis strange you should bring that up, sir,' he said.

'Of course I thought it my duty to take care of them, as some of their own parents don't, but there was a bit more than that.'

He fell silent and, after a moment, Holmes prompted him.

'A bit more?' he queried.

'You might say a big bit more,' said the harvest master. 'I was in Berkshire at the haying last summer, at Yetcham up towards Reading, and there was a boy killed there. It seemed to me that he was taken just like Bea Collins went, and I got to wondering. I thought as perhaps a maniac was following the harvest gangs looking for children.' He shook his head slowly and thoughtfully. 'But I don't know,' he said, 'I don't know.'

After another swallow of ale he said, 'Sergeant Bullington says they haven't catched anyone for Bea Collins' murder.'

'You know the sergeant?' asked Holmes.

Platt laughed, shortly. 'I knows him because I comes here each season, but I knew him long before. We was in India together.'

'You were in the Army?' I asked.

He shook his head. 'No, sir. I was in India with the Devaux company, in charge of labour on one of their plantations. That's the same Devaux brothers who has the manor here,' he explained, and I recalled seeing the brothers' names as benefactors on Miss Thorne's poster.

'So you are old friends,' remarked Holmes.

'Not what you might call friends, no, sir.

89

More old acquaintances, you might say.'

Holmes turned the conversation towards our supposed interests and Platt told us of the neck and other ceremonies that he had come across in his business.

At length Holmes asked him, 'Do you know, or know of, a harvestman called Dazzy Cooke? I was told he might be worth talking to.'

Platt looked my friend straight in the eye, with an expression that clearly showed that he did not believe one word.

'Yes,' he said. 'I knowed Dazzy Cooke. He come from hereabouts, the next village, I think. An old soldier he was. He worked with my company a time or two and he was a good harvestman when he kept away from the cider.'

'You say "was",' noted Holmes.

'I do,' said Platt. 'Dazzy Cooke hanged himself near Uphusband back in haying season.'

In the silence that followed his news, the harvest master rose from his seat and picked up his billycock and whip.

'I'm obliged to you for your hospitality, gentlemen,' he said. 'May I give you a bit of advice? There's a lot of these village people as don't like folk asking questions, however innocent the reasons, and there's some as will give wrong answers. You might call them deceivers.'

With that he tipped his whip to his billycock and was gone.

10

THE BERKSHIRE MYSTERY

'Holmes,' I said at breakfast on the next morning, 'if I understand your methods correctly—'

'One might hope so, Watson, after more than twenty years,' he interrupted.

'If I understand them correctly,' I pushed on, 'you believe that any body of data reveals patterns, by the recognition of which an investigator may deduce new facts.'

'Well done, Watson!' he cried. 'I see that two decades of association with me has not been entirely fruitless. That is a simple, but adequate, statement of one of my rules. But why do you ask, dear fellow?'

'Because,' I said, 'I scc no patterns in anything we have so far learned.'

'That, Watson,' he said, taking a slice of toast, 'is because you have failed to recognise those patterns which have emerged as well as those that have failed to materialise.'

'And they are?' I enquired.

'Really, Watson! I enumerated for Constable Russell's benefit a number of factors which led to my deductions concerning Bea Collins' death—the child's poverty, her age, the singular and unnecessary wound to the head, the presence of the corn dolly—these established that she was not the victim of a robber, a moral imbecile or someone bent on vengeance. Those deductions were based on my knowledge of the characteristic patterns of child-murder.'

'True,' I said, 'but since then we seem to have learned nothing that creates any significant pattern unless the fact that Sergeant Bullington and Mr Platt knew each other in India, and that the Lord of the Manor and his brother have business in India means anything.'

'You forget,' he said, 'the very patterns I outlined to you last evening as we returned from the vicarage. Skulls, Watson! Skulls!'

'Very well,' I conceded again, 'but we do not know the significance of them.'

'We may understand that when we have spoken to Billy Hayter,' he said. 'As to the presence of Bullington, Platt and the Devaux brothers in India, why do you regard it as insignificant?'

'I imagine,' I replied, 'that almost any village in England contains a number of persons who have served in the Army, the Civil Service or some commercial enterprise in India. Why, one might as well say that it is significant that Miss Thorne is the daughter of Indian missionaries.'

'A valid point, Watson, and one that does you credit,' he admitted. 'Our Indian involvement is so great that those who have served there are a commonplace all over the country, but that does not mean that the presence of several in Weston Stacey is insignificant.'

'But how can you tell?' I asked.

He drew from his pocket the scrap of faded blue paper that he had found in the Mayfield. 'Perhaps with this, Watson. Perhaps with this.'

I was on the point of questioning him further, but he forestalled me.

'Be so good,' he asked, 'as to ring for our host. We must arrange to be taken to the station.'

'We are going to Berkshire?' I said.

'Very good, Watson! You excel yourself this morning. We are going to Berkshire to see if your thirst for new data and fresh patterns can be assuaged.'

It was another sunny morning and, as our train rattled through the countryside, I gazed out over the wide fields of wheat coming to ripeness on either side of the line.

I was interrupted by Holmes. 'If they did not,' he remarked, 'you would not have your fine white bread, nor yet your jug of ale.'

I started, for it was one of my friend's most unnerving tricks to seem to be able to read the mind of a companion. 'How do you do it, Holmes?' I asked.

'Simplicity itself,' he replied. 'As we left the station you glanced at your newspaper, but it failed to interest you and you laid it aside. You made yourself comfortable in your seat and began to watch the passing landscape with a slight but broadening smile. You were, I believe, congratulating yourself on living in a country so agriculturally rich and observing to yourself that this splendid season of sunshine will bring a bumper harvest, barring a meteorological disaster. But then you turned away from the window and your smile disappeared. After a slight frown you picked up your newspaper again. It was then that I was sure you had recalled that the bringing in of England's harvest is partly the business of little children like Bea or our friend Alice. That was the point at which I interrupted.'

'Really, Holmes!' I exclaimed. 'The Reverend Trentham is right. In another age they would have burned you!'

He smiled thinly without further comment and I turned back to my newspaper.

Holmes had wired ahead to the police at Yetcham and an inspector met us at the little station.

'The superintendent has come down from Reading,' he said as he introduced himself. 'He wishes to meet you in person, Mr Holmes, and to have the advantage of any advice which you may give upon the matter.'

His remark cheered us both. Too often we had experienced downright hostility from local officers when pursuing an enquiry and it was pleasing to know that we might now expect some co-operation. Superintendent Godden awaited us at the police station and shook us warmly by the hand. He was a wide-shouldered, fresh-faced man with a heavy, fair moustache and his soft drawl revealed him to be a local man.

'Mr Holmes!' he said. 'May I say what a pleasure it is to meet you and your colleague. If I understand your telegram, you're interested in the case of Joseph Baker?'

'If that is the child who was murdered during the hay harvest, yes,' confirmed Holmes. 'I am engaged on an enquiry into what may be a similar matter and we may be able to assist each other.'

'I should welcome any assistance you could give, Mr Holmes,' said the Superintendent, 'for between you and me we are no further forward in this affair than the day the lad was discovered.'

'Perhaps, then,' said Holmes, 'you will be good enough to outline the facts of the boy's death, Superintendent.'

A constable was told off to produce tea and we settled in the inspector's office to hear the superintendent's recital of the facts.

'Joseph Baker,' he began, 'was twelve years old, the son of a labourer at one of the farms hereabouts. In June of last year the haymaking was on and he was employed by a gangmaster, one Albert Platt, to assist in the hayfields. I understand that he did so from the beginning of haymaking without complaint by him nor against him. On 16th June, the last hay was being cut at Three Winds Farm and he was on the field as usual. At the day's end, as the last cart was leaving, he told his workmates as he was not following the cart to the yard, as he was going straight home.'

'What time of day was this?' enquired Holmes.

'It was about half-past six,' said the superintendent. 'So far as we can guess,' he went on, 'the lad left the hayfield shortly after the last cart and set out on his road home.'

He stood up and drew our attention to a large map of the district which was pinned on the wall. 'Here in the middle is Yetcham,' he said, 'and here to the left is Three Winds Farm with the hayfield in question lying right out on its western edge. Now left again, along this road here, is a little group of cottages at a place called Scotchman's Crossing. That was where young Joseph and his family lived. You can see that the road from Three Winds drops down around this little bit of hill and he wouldn't have gone by the road. There is a well-used path across this big meadow here,' and he pointed, 'which would have taken him home shorter.'

I congratulated myself that I was beginning to see the similarities between the Berkshire boy's death and that of Bea Collins.

'When he hadn't come home after dark,'

continued the superintendent, 'his people went out looking for him. They found him here,' he said, pointing a finger at the centre of the large meadow on the map.

'On or near the path across that meadow?' asked Holmes.

'Beside the path,' said the superintendent, 'right in the middle of Fair Meadow, as it is known.'

'Precisely how was he lying?' asked Holmes.

Superintendent Godden shook his head. 'That I cannot tell you for sure. Being found by his parents and them being distressed he had been moved before any officer saw him, but his father said he was laid as though asleep upon his back. Both his hands was on his chest, holding a corn dolly.'

'A corn dolly?' I exclaimed but Holmes remained silent.

'That's right, Doctor,' said the superintendent. 'I don't know if you'll know what they are.'

'Oh, I know them,' I said. 'I was raised in an agricultural county.'

'How had the boy died?' interjected Holmes.

'He was strangled,' said the superintendent, 'choked with a cloth or something like.'

'Was the cloth found?' asked my friend.

'No, sir. We thought it might be a labourer's neck-cloth and they all wears them.'

Holmes nodded. 'Was there any other injury

to the boy?'

'He had an injury to the head,' replied the police officer. 'At first we thought as he'd struck his head against a stone, but when it was examined it proved to be a deliberate blow. It was the surgeon's opinion that he was struck senseless and then strangled.'

'Does the surgeon have any opinion as to the weapon with which the boy was struck?'

'He did say as it was unusual, Mr Holmes. He thought it was a narrow metal object with a taper to it and an oblong end. He thought maybe a tool of some kind, but we haven't been able to determine what kind.'

'Might it have been a cordwainer's punch?' I asked, recalling our discussion with PC Russell.

'It might, Doctor,' said the police officer, 'but we found none near the body nor in the possession of any suspect and we don't even have a cobbler in the village. Still, if it was a local man who did it, I dare say that little weapon might still be tucked away in his cottage.'

'You say a local man,' said Holmes. 'Have you any particular reason to think it was a man and a local one?'

'I say a man because of the blow to the head. That was struck forcibly and downwards at the back of the boy's head. That says to me that it was a man, a large youth, or at a stretch a strong woman. Local, I says, because it was

98

someone who knew the short-cut to Scotchman's Crossing and seemed to know as the boy would go that way.'

Holmes nodded. 'Eminently reasonable,' he said. 'Tell me, was there no indication that this is the work of a defective or a moral imbecile?'

'None at all.'

'And was the area where the body was found searched?'

The superintendent smiled. 'I knew you'd ask that, Mr Holmes. Soon as I knew you were coming I said to my inspector, "He'll want to know what we found in the search."'

He gestured to his inspector who lifted a cardboard box down from a shelf, passing it to his superior. The superintendent lifted the lid and showed us the contents—a headless toy soldier made of lead, a disc of plain metal about the size of a half-crown piece and a scrap of coarse blue paper.

'These were all found within a few feet of where the boy lay. Of course, it is a footpath and there's no saying as they were dropped by the boy or the killer, but we searched the whole path and found nought else.'

Holmes nodded over the contents of the box, then drew out the scrap of paper. He touched a long finger to it then applied the finger to his tongue.

'Sugar,' he stated.

'I should have told you, Mr Holmes,' said the superintendent, 'that there was two sugar cubes still wrapped in it when we found it.'

Holmes nodded and picked up the metal disc. He drew out his lens and applied it to the artefact then looked up.

'Do you know what this is?' he enquired.

Both officers shook their heads. 'We have had a number of engineers look at it,' said the inspector. 'They have all said that they couldn't make it out to be anything in particular. Mostly they said as it looked like the pieces left over when holes are stamped in something.'

Holmes lifted the disc to his nostrils. 'And faintly perfumed,' he remarked, tossing the piece back into the box.

'You have done very well, gentlemen,' he said. 'Now let me explain to you where my interest in this matter lies.'

Briefly he set out the facts of the Weston Stacey killing, leaving out the source of our information and the question of Sergeant Bullington's strange conduct. The two Berkshire officers listened in silence until he was done.

'Why,' said the superintendent when Holmes' recital was finished, 'it must be the same man, for sure!'

'But you,' said Holmes, 'have postulated a local killer and for the same reasons it might be said that our murderer is local to Weston Stacey.'

His audience looked dumbfounded and he

smiled thinly. 'It is in the highest degree unlikely that two such individual killings are the work of two separate persons. Consequently we must consider that the killers are connected in some way or that both crimes are the work of the same person. For that reason, Superintendent, I shall be grateful if you will seek someone in Yetcham who has connections with Weston Stacey. You may communicate with me at the John Barleycorn inn at Weston but you had best use the assumed name under which they know me there,' and he gave it.

He stood up from his chair. 'I am grateful to you,' he said, 'for supplying me with extra data. With your help I believe that this ugly affair can be brought to a successful conclusion. Perhaps you would assist me in one more small point.'

'Of course, sir.'

'Then perhaps you will be good enough to confirm that the Fair Meadow is planted with wheat this year?'

'Well, yes,' said the Inspector, 'but how come you know that, Mr Holmes?'

'It was merely,' said my friend, 'a logical deduction. Good afternoon, gentlemen.'

11

MASTER HAYTER'S NARRATIVE

'Well, Watson,' said Holmes as we settled ourselves in our compartment for the journey back to Weston Stacey, 'what did you make of the superintendent's data?'

'It was abundantly clear,' I replied 'that the two matters are related—the use of a curious weapon, the strangulation, the waylaying of the child on a footpath, the corn dolly—all these things are identical.'

'True,' he said, 'and one should not forget the sugar cubes nor yet the metal disc. What do you make of the disc, Watson?'

I had been puzzling about that artefact ever since the superintendent had revealed it to us. I shook my head. 'I do not know,' I said. 'You evidently regard it as significant, but might it not be merely an object fallen from someone's pocket along that path? After all, it would be easy to relate the broken toy soldier to the dead boy, but there is no way to establish that they are related.'

'Very good, Watson,' he said, 'and your reasoning may be correct. There may be numbers of persons in Yetcham who habitually carry blank metal discs in their pockets and often drop them. No doubt when the superintendent finds one he will be able to ask him why the disc is faintly perfumed.'

'Holmes,' I said, 'if you are going to pour sarcasm on—'

He flung up a hand. 'I apologise, dear fellow. You have the right of it. I cannot establish a connection between the metal disc and the boy's death. On the other hand, the local police searched the entire path and found only three items—the broken soldier which may well have been accidentally dropped or may have belonged to the dead boy, the sugar cubes which, unless I am gravely mistaken, are a significant key to the entire mystery, and the metal disc which has no apparent significance apart from the fact that it smells of perfume rather than machine oil. I will not theorise so far ahead of the data as to state that the disc is significant, but I believe that it may be as important as the sugar cubes or the name of the field.'

His ready apology threw me off guard, so that I was slow to realise the amount of opinion he had crammed into his remarks. By the time I had grasped the content and was about to question him about the sugar cubes he had composed himself in his corner of the compartment, closed his eyes and to all intents and purposes seemed to be asleep.

The station trap deposited us outside the John Barleycorn, where we found our little friend Alice playing on the grass. She sprang up as we climbed down from the trap and ran across to us.

'Billy Hayter and his Dad are back from harvesting,' she said. 'You asked me to keep an eye out.'

'We did indeed,' said Holmes, and slipped the child a coin. 'Now there's another of those if you will show us the way to Billy Hayter's cottage.'

In a very short time we stood at the Hayters' gate, where Holmes paid his debt to our guide and she skipped away.

A man in middle years and a boy of about twelve were seated on a bench in the trim little cottage garden. That both were harvesters was obvious from the brick-red skin of their faces and forearms.

'Mr Hayter?' called Holmes from the gate.

The man got up and walked to the fence, the boy following. 'That's me, sir,' he said. 'What can I do for you?'

'We were wondering if we might have a word or two with Billy,' said Holmes.

'With Billy?' said his father. 'He ain't in no trouble. Leastways, not hereabouts. We've only last night come back from harvesting in Somerset. He ain't been up to anything here.'

'No, no trouble, Mr Hayter,' said Holmes, shaking his head. 'We understand that, before he went away, Billy saw something unusual at the Buckstone and we would be grateful for the chance to hear him tell about it.'

104

'Something unusual, you calls it!' exclaimed Hayter. 'More like a load of old nonsense. That's why I took him harvesting, to get such silly notions out of his head.'

'Perhaps I should explain,' said Holmes, 'that my friend and I are staying in the village because we are interested in the old songs and stories and the things that people used to believe. It seemed to us that Billy might have a very fine ghost story to tell and, of course, we would be willing to pay for his time in telling it.'

The mention of money seemed to soften the elder Hayter's attitude. He swung the gate open and invited us into his garden, calling to his wife inside the cottage to bring tea.

'Now then, Billy,' he commanded his son, 'you tell these gentlemen what you told me and your mother about what you saw by the Buckstone.'

The boy twisted his large hands together with embarrassment. 'Where is the Buckstone?' encouraged Holmes.

Billy twisted and pointed. 'Over there,' he said. 'There's a path across the Mayfield and on the other side there's trees. The Buckstone is there in them trees.'

'And what is it?' asked Holmes.

'It's a big old stone, taller than a man, that's been there for ever so long.'

'It's one of them old stones like you can see at Avebury,' interrupted his father, 'if you

105

knows Avebury, gentlemen. They was put here generations ago. Vicar says as the old people in them days used to pray at them.'

Holmes nodded. 'And when was it you saw something by the Buckstone?' he asked the boy.

The boy, whose way of life required no diary more accurate than the passing seasons, screwed up his face and thought hard.

'It was weeks ago,' he said, 'before me and my Dad went to Somerset, maybe about the end of haymaking. I went out one night, just walking out like.'

Holmes' lips silently formed the word 'poaching' so that only I could see, but he nodded encouragement to our informant. 'What time of night was it?' he asked.

'I can't rightly say only that 'twas well after moonrise. I remember that it was moonlight, bright and clear. I was going over the Mayfield. I don't like going there at night, past where little Bea was killed, but it was as bright as day and I thought no harm. I had gone across the top of the Mayfield and was coming down towards the wood where the Buckstone is when I heard a noise.'

'What sort of noise?' asked Holmes.

' 'Twas a sort of singing, sir, though not much like any song I ever did hear.'

'Was it one voice or many?'

'It seemed like only one voice, sir, singing on its own with no instrument nor nothing with it.'

'Could you hear any words?' asked my friend.

The boy shook his head. 'It wasn't words, sir just noises, like. Nothing I could understand.'

'So what did you do?'

'Well, sir, I wondered who was out in the moonlight singing, so I went a bit quiet like into the trees by the Buckstone. 'Tis very dark about the stone, sir. The trees is close overhead. Well, I got myself into the bushes and looked to see what was happening and who was making that noise.'

'And what did you see?'

'Well, when my eyes was used to the dark under the trees, I could see as someone was moving about at the back of the Buckstone. There's a little old pool there, behind the stone, and I could see something moving against the water.'

'And what was it?' asked Holmes. 'Did you get a good look?'

The boy shook his head again and spoke slowly as if reluctant to recall his experience. 'If you was to ask me an hundred times, sir, I couldn't say what it was I saw, for I never saw nothing like it before nor since. It was big, tall, as tall as the stone, nearly, and it was sort of moving about from side to side behind the stone, almost like it was dancing and all the time it kept making that singing sort of noise.'

'Did you not see—' I began, but Holmes forestalled me with a raised hand.

'Did you not see it more clearly at any point?' he asked, flashing me a stern warning glance for he had rightly deduced that I was about to ask about the skulls.

'Just the once, sir. For a moment. It strayed a bit farther from the stone and there was a little patch of moonlight. Then I saw it for just a second the moonlight—and I wouldn't want to see it no longer.'

'Why is that?' asked Holmes.

'It was horrible, sir—horrible like nothing I'd ever seen before. It had a great mouth full of teeth and big staring eyes and a lot of hair hanging about its shoulders. I tell you truly, sir, that frightened me. I wasn't frightened when I thought it was just a big old animal of some kind, but that was something I'd never seen, something horrible.'

He shuddered in the hot afternoon at the recollection.

'It had long hair about its head,' said Holmes. 'What was its body covered in?'

'That's how I knew it wasn't an animal, sir. It had a cloak or something wrapped about it and hanging at its neck was little skulls.'

'Skulls!' I exclaimed.

'Were they animal skulls?' asked Holmes.

'No, sir. I seen all sorts of animal skulls and birds, sir—foxes, rabbits, crows and that—old Wiggin the Devauxs' gamekeeper hangs all kinds up on a rack by his cottage in the woods, but these wasn't none of them. These was little skulls like on the gravestones in the churchyard, like skulls of people.'

'You say that you were frightened when you saw that it was not an animal,' said Holmes. 'What did you think it was?'

'For all I knowed, sir, it could have been the Devil himself. I just took off out of the bushes and I ran. I went across the Mayfield and I ran hard as I knew.'

'And did it follow you?'

'Not so as I knew, sir. When I got across the Mayfield I stopped for breath and looked after me, but it wasn't coming.'

'Could you still hear it singing?'

'No, sir. It stopped that as soon as I ran and I never heard it again.'

Holmes drew a coin from his pocket and presented it to the boy. Rising from the bench where we had been sitting, he stepped across to the elder Hayter and drew him away into conversation by the gate. I saw money change hands then Holmes thanked Hayter and his son and opened the gate.

'Let us be about our business,' he said and I followed him down the lane.

'That was extremely strange,' I remarked as I caught up with his long stride.

'Indeed,' he remarked, 'but now we have our skulls, Watson, unless you are prepared to disbelieve the boy.'

'Oh no,' I said. 'I am sure that he was telling the truth as he understood it. But what can he have seen? Might he have been hallucinating?'

'He might, Watson, but I very much doubt if he was.'

'What did you say to his father?' I asked.

'I advised him to take his son away from Weston Stacey for the time being. Hayter complained that they had returned from Somerset for the local harvest which will soon commence. I had to buy out the harvest earnings of man and boy, but I believe it is safer for Billy Hayter to be away from here until the harvest ends.'

'Why so?' I enquired.

'Because he is the obvious choice as the next victim.'

12

THE DEVIL'S WIND

'It came at me from nowhere—out of the sky, like—a-whirling and a-crackling and a-sparking like it was Guy Fawkes.'

Holmes and I had made our way back to the John Barleycorn and taken our dinner, followed by a drink at our usual table in the bar. We had not been long seated when the outer door banged wide and a man staggered in.

As the newcomer hobbled to the bar,

demanding brandy, I recognised him as one of the labourers I associated with the singing of the John Barleycorn ballad each night. I believed his name to be Sam West. Holmes left his seat and joined the small crowd that was gathering around West and I followed.

Closer to the man I could see that he was showing all the symptoms of a severe shock. I could not let my assumed identity frustrate my duties as a doctor, and thrust into the little group to assist the man.

'I am a doctor!' I called. 'Now stand away and give the poor fellow some air!'

With the assistance of Holmes I managed to help the man to a corner settle and let him lie full length on the seat, making a pillow for him of my jacket. Holmes fetched a large brandy from the bar.

As West gulped gratefully at the brandy I observed him. My first diagnosis had been correct. His face was deadly pale and his eyes starting, his extremities icy cold despite the warmth of the evening and his pulse fluttering.

'This man has been absolutely terrified by something,' I observed to Holmes in a low tone.

The spirit seemed to calm the man a little and to bring a slight colour to his cheeks. He tried to sit up, but I pressed him back and Holmes bent close to him.

'Tell me,' said Holmes, 'what is it that has so frightened you?'

It is one of Holmes' most astonishing characteristics that, when he chooses to do so, he can calm fractious children, hysterical women or frightened men by the mere sound of his voice. In that mode he seems to have an almost hypnotic effect and so it was with West.

He lay back on the settle and his ragged breathing eased. 'I were coming across the Mayfield,' he said. 'You know where that is, sir?'

Holmes nodded and the man continued.

'I were coming across the Mayfield and I heard a noise, like a buzzing, whirring sort of thing. I thought of bees and I looked about to see. First of all I couldn't see a thing, but after a moment or two I saw something fluttering across the hillside.'

He paused and we waited.

'I couldn't see what it was. It was flickering and dancing over the wheat like no more than a smudge of smoke, but it was making this here buzzing sort of noise. Then I seed as it were coming straight at me and I took to running, but I wasn't nowhere fast enough. Before I was many yards it was on top of me and all about me. It was a-buzzing and a-crackling at me from every side, so as I didn't know where to turn, and I could hardly see anything of it, it was always just a-whizzing and a-whirling in the air, but there was sparks and crackling and all my hair stood up and sparked.'

His breathing had become agitated again and he paused. Holmes offered him another brandy which he snatched at and swallowed at two gulps before continuing.

'I thought I was dead, for sure,' he went on. 'I ran into the wheat so as it shouldn't find me, but it kept after me, whirling and a-buzzing about me, sparking and cracking like fire crackers and humming like a swarm of bees. I fell down and lay all on the ground and I thought my time was come. I was certain sure that I was a goner and I laid on the ground saying the Lord's Prayer, but I could barely put my tongue to it, and all the time that thing was whirring and swooshing in the corn about me, beating it flat to the ground as though it would get at me and my hair was sparking and flames of blue was running over my hands.'

He paused again to catch his breath. His delivery had become more excited and his eyes wider and staring, as though he looked beyond us to a vision of the phenomenon that had attacked him.

'What did you believe it was?' asked Holmes.

'What was it, sir? Why it were the Devil—that's what! I lay on that old field in fear for my immortal soul, sir, for I knew the Devil had sent his wind from Hell to fetch me.'

Now he pulled himself up on the settle and addressed himself to the little crowd of labourers huddled behind us. 'That was the Devil, I say. He come for me as he will come for all of us, and you all knows why because we has done his work and put ourselves in his power. We are dead men—every one—all dead and damned for ever for what we let be done.'

He was growing more excited and less coherent by the minute. I asked Holmes to care for the man while I went rapidly to my room and returned with a strong sleeping draught from my medical bag. Once I had administered it in a further measure of brandy I called on the assistance of those around us.

'This poor fellow has evidently had a serious fright,' I said. 'I have given him something that will make him sleep. Perhaps some of you would be good enough to help him to his home and see him settled. He will not give you any trouble now.'

Three or four men came forwards and lifted my patient, gently bearing him out of the door. The sleeping powder and raw brandy had taken quick effect and he was already drowsy. As he was carried out the last I heard of him was a faint mumble, 'That was the Devil come for me as he will come for us all because we done his work.'

Once West had been taken out the drinkers drifted back to their seats though it was evident that they were still excitedly discussing and apparently arguing about West's strange appearance and narrative. More than once I thought that I had caught a furtive glance in our direction, as though they were connecting Holmes and me with the extraordinary event.

Holmes, however, remained silent for some time after we had resumed our seats. I waited until he had filled his pipe and smoked it through before breaking the silence.

'That man was severely shocked,' I remarked.

'So you said, Watson, and I agree with you.'

'But what can have happened to him?' I asked.

Holmes knocked out his pipe against the heel of his boot. 'I think you may take it,' he said, 'that he was not the victim of a personal attack by the Devil.'

'And that's another thing,' I continued. 'What is all this about the Devil? One would think we were living in the Middle Ages, not the early years of the twentieth century.'

'You have already seen that superstition and traditional belief are strong in this area,' said my friend. 'When the ignorant come across phenomena which they do not understand and which frighten them, they attribute them to the Devil. Scientists are very similar—they attribute them to unlikely and unprovable causes which are never established by observation or experiment.'

'But what did that man see?'

'In the Middle Ages,' said Holmes, 'it would, I think, have been called a "Mowing Devil"—a fiend which laid the corn of farmers' fields flat in great circles. Nowadays men of science have equally unlikely explanations. If they cannot attribute the circles to the work of hooligans, they postulate nonsensical theories about the roots of the grain being weakened by circles of toadstool spores in the earth, or the corn being flattened by the mating rituals of hedgehogs. I sometimes think that there is nothing so creative as the mind of a man of science who has been cornered by an event which his science cannot explain.'

'Then you believe what West told us?'

'Most certainly,' he said. 'I have told you before, Watson, in the absence of any contrary indications it is as well to believe the account given by a witness.'

'Then what was it that overtook him?'

'I believe,' he said, 'that a wise old man called Erasmus Darwin explained the matter, more than a hundred years ago. A friend wrote to him, drawing his attention to the appearance of flattened circles in fields of crops. He replied to the effect that, though he had never seen one, he imagined that they would be caused by some kind of electrically charged atmosphere discharging itself to the ground. Did you not note that West's description, although unscientific, was entirely compatible with Darwin's theory?'

'Then you believe it is an entirely natural manifestation?'

'Oh, absolutely,' he said, 'and interesting

enough, but what is ten times more interesting is the reaction of poor West. Why does he believe so strongly that he and his fellows will be punished for doing the Devil's work? What Devil's work have they done?'

'You mean,' I said, 'that he was referring to some common bond of guilt among them?'

'Precisely, Watson. Furthermore, during your absence I overheard his friends discussing his fears. One of them—it was the singer, I think—expressed the view that West was a danger to them all and they must meet tonight to deal with the problem.'

'Then they are some kind of confederates?'

'So it would seem, Watson, and I believe it would be of use to our enquiry to attend their meeting, though not, perhaps, in a way which would draw attention to our presence. Perhaps, before closing time, you will be good enough to slip upstairs and return with our pistols.'

'You think wc may come into danger?' I asked.

'Something,' he said, 'has killed a drunken labourer, whether by murder or by driving him to suicide, and has strangled two children. I have every reason to believe that West has frightened that something and that it will strike back—soon.'

'We are going to intervene?'

'We are going to observe, Watson, but intervention may well be forced upon us. Hence my request for the revolvers.'

I did as he had asked and we sat together in silence. Holmes smoked his pipe steadily and kept a wary eye on the group of singers. Towards closing time we had our regular visit from Sergeant Bullington. Usually he paced around the room, exchanging only a few curt remarks with the labourers, but I noticed that on this occasion he spent some minutes standing by their table in converse with them.

As he left, he paused by our table.

'Good evening, gentlemen,' he said. 'I must thank you, Doctor, for looking after old West. I had not realised that you were a medical man.'

'I am on holiday,' I said, 'as you know, but a doctor's duty, like a policeman's, must be done when it is needed. How is the poor fellow?'

'His wife says he is sleeping soundly on the draft you gave him, Doctor.'

'I was astonished by his account of his experience,' I said.

'Oh, you shouldn't take too much notice of that kind of thing,' said the sergeant. 'It's been another hot day and, if I know West, he'll have been well at the cider at dinner-time. He might have seen anything. I shouldn't think it's one for your collection of folklore.'

He tipped his helmet and bade us goodnight. A few minutes later our landlord called 'Last orders!' and there was no delaying. The bar emptied rapidly, as though all present had other, urgent, business.

As the publican was about to bolt the front door, Holmes strolled across.

'I would be grateful,' he said, 'if you will be kind enough to leave the back door open for us. We both fancy taking a little air before we turn in.'

We were let out into the village street, which was brightly moonlit, so that we could see that it was quite empty. There were none of the young labourers who usually loitered for a few minutes after the inn had closed.

Holmes strode away rapidly.

'Come, Watson!' he commanded. 'The game's afoot!'

13

THE TAKING OF SUGAR

Holmes made a vigorous pace along the deserted street and out of the village. I was hard put to it to keep up with his long strides, and was soon perspiring freely in the warm night.

The high moon shed a bright light across fields and coppices, turning everything to misleading shades of silver and grey so that at first I did not recognise the route which Holmes had taken, but gradually I realised that he seemed to be making towards Buckstone, either by the lane which served the hamlet or perhaps by the short-cut across the Mayfield.

He ended my doubts by leaping the stile at the corner of the Mayfield. At the bottom of the short-cut he paused and took his watch from his pocket, turning its face to the moon.

'We are, I think, so far ahead of them that we shall readily hear them coming. If you have cigarettes about you, Watson, we may smoke them here, whereas we may not do so once we are in hiding.'

I understood this only far enough to take out my cigarette case. We smoked in silence for a moment, then my curiosity overcame me.

'Who, precisely, are we expecting?' I enquired.

'It has been evident from the first that these killings are the work of a group,' he said, 'and if there were any doubt it was dispelled by the fear into which a perfectly natural, if unusual, phenomenon threw the man West. His guilt was not only writ large upon his face, he called to his fellows, warning them that they had done the Devil's work and should suffer his vengeance.'

I nodded. 'Then the farm labourers are mixed up in the killings?' I said.

'Indubitably,' he said. 'Though they are led by some person or persons who are certainly not labourers—'

'And what do you expect of the labourers now?' I asked.

'While you fetched your medical bag, I heard those crowded around me mutter among themselves. They were alarmed by West's remarks, afraid that he might give something away. They spoke of meeting urgently tonight to deal with the matter.'

'And where will they meet?'

'Unless I miss my guess, at the Buckstone. Come, Watson!'

We ground out our cigarettes and crossed the field, passing the little memorial to Bea Collins, and followed the path into the trees beyond. Here, despite the bright moon, it was almost pitch dark, the ancient trees forming a thick canopy overhead which admitted only occasional thin beams of light.

We were able to see the Buckstone, standing back under the trees, almost like a tall, broad, hulking human figure. In front of it a patch of flat ground bore traces of ash within a circle of small stones. Holmes stood and peered about him in the gloom, pointing at last with his stick.

'A seat in the stalls, I think, Watson, behind the undergrowth there. It is thick enough to show that nobody passes that way and to conceal us.'

We wormed our way cautiously under the thick clumps of bushes, carefully drawing the branches back behind us to conceal our passage. At length we found a kind of natural chamber or vault under the bushes, where we could sprawl at length and maintain some kind of observation on the area in front of the ancient stone.

Before us lay the flat space in front of the Buckstone, which stood to our left in front of a clump of undergrowth such as that which concealed us. A mephitic odour drifting from our right made me aware of the presence of stagnant water. Straining my eyes in the gloom, I saw that there was a pool in that direction. Faint gleams of light marked its surface and a cloud of insects buzzed above its noisome water.

We had not long settled into our positions when we heard voices approaching from the direction of the Mayfield. Soon footsteps sounded in the undergrowth and a number of figures entered the space in front of the stone. Despite our limited vision, we could see that they were eight or ten of the village labourers and that among them was the man West. He was being jostled by his companions, who squatted in two parallel lines before the Buckstone, leaving West alone in the centre. They chatted quietly among themselves, though I noted that none of them lit a pipe or cigarette, despite the mephitic reek of the stagnant pool.

Suddenly a voice spoke from behind the Buckstone, and although we were unable to hear the words it was evidently a command, for the group straightened its two facing lines and sat silent. With a rustle of bushes a figure slipped around the old stone and stood immediately in front of it, silhouetted against the grey stone. It was a tall man draped from head to heel in a long black cowl, similar to a monk's garb and provided with a hood which was drawn forward so as to completely conceal the face in its shadows. The figure spoke again and held forward both its hands with a vessel of some kind which glinted like silver in the gloom. It appeared to be intoning some incantation over the bowl.

The two lines of men sat on their haunches while the robed figure moved first along the left-hand line, then along the right. In front of each man it paused and offered the bowl while the kneeling man took something from the bowl and placed it in his mouth. I was uneasily aware that I was watching some kind of parody of Holy Communion.

'Consecrated sugar!' whispered Holmes, very quietly. 'I was right, after all!'

When both lines had been served the figure retreated once more to the stone, and stood in front of it, placing the silver vessel at its feet. A further announcement or command of some length came from the cowled man, during which his right hand was pointed at West, who still knelt alone between the lines and who had received no offering from the bowl.

A short silence followed, then one of the kneeling men spoke and though we could not distinguish his words it was evident that they were urgent and perhaps angry. The robed man nodded and another of the labourers spoke, then another, until each in turn had had their say. Now the cowled leader spoke again, sweeping his arms around as though in invocation to the group. One after another the kneeling labourers each raised his right hand.

'They have found him guilty,' whispered Holmes. 'Be ready with your pistol, Watson!'

The black-robed figure spoke again, intoning some solemn statement, and I heard West groan aloud. Another voice was heard, undoubtedly the voice of the singer from the village inn. Slowly he sang the opening of his song:

'There were three men came out of the West,
    their fortune for to try,
And these three men swore a solemn oath
    John Barleycorn should die.'

Hearing the old ballad every night at the inn had made me increasingly aware of the savage imagery within it, but those two lines sung in the reeking gloom beneath the trees sounded like the very voice of death. Poor West shrieked aloud and flung his hands to his face.

'Do not shoot to kill, Watson, unless you must,' whispered my friend. 'Our object is to get West and ourselves out of here alive.'

I admit that I was not very hopeful of success, but I had been in a good many tight spots with

Holmes and I was certainly prepared to try a rescue. I slipped my pistol from my pocket and eased my limbs to be ready for movement.

The singer's voice had ended and the only sound was of West sobbing unrestrainedly. Holmes began to move forward and I made to follow him when a further sound behind the Buckstone brought a new character on to the gloomy stage before us. Holmes clamped a commanding hand on my arm and we crouched to await this new development.

If the appearance of the black-robed man had been sinister, the figure that now stepped from the shadow by the stone was terrifying. Taller than a tall man and with a mane of hair that hung around its shoulders, the thing had two large eyes that glowed even in the faint light of the little clearing. It was clothed from neck to heel in a coloured and ornamented robe whose decorations caught the little light and sparkled and on either side of its neck there hung two small white objects which I knew at once were the skulls of small children. The hideous thing writhed and undulated before the ancient stone emitting a piercing cry in a weird, ululating tone. If it was language it was not any tongue that I understood, but the effect on the group around it was immediate. One and all they flung their foreheads to the ground, abasing themselves like Mohammedans at prayer, while emitting some gibberish chant, even the cowled priest figure bending with the rest.

The wretched West's terrified sobs gave way to a high hopeless wail of fear, and I confess that the piercing cries of the skull-bedizened creature, the chanting of its acolytes and West's hysterical wailing made my blood run cold.

The scene was literally unearthly, as though some fiend from the very Pit had stepped into this dark corner of England and infected it with the contagion of Hell. I could not fathom the slaughterous madness that ran in the minds of the men prostrated before this monstrous being, and as to the nature of the creature itself I could make no sensible guess. The sweat on my brow turned to ice as I watched the demonic madness being played out in the darkened clearing.

At the same time, the blasphemous parody of a Christian sacrament and the seeming imitation of some Eastern ceremony by this band of executioners—for there was now no possible doubt of their nature—had filled me with a deep anger and loathing. I was more than ready to act and only waited my friend's command. I was aware that our two pistols would not, in themselves, protect us from the anger of the fanatics before us if we interrupted their vile ceremonial. Were the entire crowd to rush us, we would be hard put to it to lay them all low while making our escape from the undergrowth, let alone to create a way of escape for West, but I had been in many a tight spot alongside Sherlock Holmes and we had both survived. What is more, I had never been so convinced of the absolute evil of the opposition. I was quite determined that if we could not effect Holmes' plan, then we should sell ourselves very dearly in the attempt.

'I think,' he whispered, 'it is time that we intervened, Watson.'

Together we fired a rapid fusillade across the little clearing.

14

A BRACING WALK HOME

As we fired, the chanting ended abruptly. We could hear our bullets whine under the trees, see some of them strike sparks from the upper part of the Buckstone and hear them ricochet away into the darkness. The blasphemous revellers in front of the stone had been struck dumb with surprise.

West was the first to move. Whether he perceived his chance to escape or whether his dazed wits had finally cracked I know not, but he plunged away into the darkness, shrieking, ' 'Tis the Devil! He has come for his own, just as I told you!'

His headlong run took him straight towards the reeking pool and for a moment I feared that he had escaped death at the hands of his fellows to meet it in the stinking sludge, but he was either aware or careless of the pool's depth, for he plunged across it still running, revealing it to be little more than ankle deep.

The splash as West ran across the pool seemed to break the spell that our gunfire had imposed. A handful of his fellows sprang up and ran after him while the others clambered cautiously to their feet. Of the skull-draped creature in the glittering robe I could see nothing; it had disappeared back behind the stone as soon as we began firing, but the cowled man still squatted by the stone.

'After them!' he ordered. 'There's men in the bushes!'

They were understandably unwilling to plunge into the black undergrowth against an unknown number of men armed with pistols, and we took the opportunity to weaken their resolve by loosing a few more shots close over their heads before following West's example and plunging away through the brush.

The shots deterred them for only a moment. The sound of our passage through the bushes must have made them realise that there was no large number of us and it had dawned on them that we had not shot to kill. With the cowled priest still snarling execrations and commands, they came after us.

128

A particularly heavy stand of brambles bade fair to wreck our escape, for it could not be negotiated quickly nor was there time to seek a way round it. We had paused momentarily before it when the first of our pursuers plunged out of the undergrowth behind us.

When they were so close behind us that further flight was pointless, Holmes and I turned at bay. One of the ruffians butted me in the stomach with his head, sending me sprawling, and improved the moment by kicking me as I attempted to rise, while the remainder, led by the cowled man, concentrated their efforts on Holmes.

I lurched to my knees, gasping for breath and groping for my pistol and, a second later, something whirred in front of my face and I felt my throat gripped as though in a vice. I realised that some kind of ligature had been wrapped around my neck and I clutched at it to frcc mysclf, but it was bcing drawn inexorably tighter by my attacker. Winded as I was before the strangulation began, I knew that I could not survive this assault for very long.

As we rolled on the ground, my flailing hand came in contact with my pistol and, without paying much mind to Holmes' requirement not to kill or injure, I twisted the gun over my shoulder and pulled the trigger. My assailant shrieked and I felt the pressure on my throat relax. I rolled away from him, clawing the cloth away from my bruised throat.

For moments I was completely disorientated, my lungs heaving and my head swimming. When my senses were a little restored I stumbled to my feet and looked to assist my friend. He had drawn the blade of his swordstick and was holding the cowled man and two of his henchmen at bay, while two more lay on the ground.

My lungs heaving, my breath rasping in my aching throat and coloured spots dancing before my eyes, I stumbled about trying to find a point from which I might safely fire at Holmes' attackers, but their struggle was so closely involved that I saw no opportunity. In the event I should have trusted more to my friend's oriental fighting skills, for one of his assailants soon spun out of the battle and dropped senseless at the foot of a tree while another disengaged and fled into the depths of the wood, leaving Holmes to grapple with the cowled priest.

Deserted by his henchmen, the cowled man attacked my friend with the greater fury, wielding some kind of long staff, but I knew that Holmes was a match for almost any man alive in a straightforward man-to-man conflict. As his attacker swung at Holmes' head with his staff, my friend's swordstick flashed up in his right hand to intercept and hold the blow, while with his left hand he delivered a tremendous blow to his opponent's face. I knew that Holmes had studied under one of

Europe's greatest masters of the sword, and I had heard professional prize-fighters express the view that he might have made a good living in the ring. The combination of his two refined skills was deadly.

In a second it was all over. The hooded man collapsed in a heap and Holmes slid his swordstick blade back into its sheath.

'Come, Watson,' he said, straightening the collar of his linen coat. 'I rather think that we should not dawdle here.'

Dawdle we did not, but I could not manage any great speed. The night's injuries to my stomach and throat left me wincing and gasping as we made our way out of the wood, and Holmes was forced to turn and wait for me a number of times.

'You must go on without me, Holmes,' I wheezed on one of these occasions.

'Nonsense!' he said. 'We are nearly at the edge of the wood—'

'And any minute now those lunatics will regroup and come after us,' I interrupted him. 'Leave me here with the pistols, while you go for help.'

'I shall do no such thing,' he said. 'In the first place I would rather avoid a midnight gun battle in the Wiltshire countryside if possible, and in the second, I am not at all sure whence we might summon help in Weston Stacey.'

We emerged from the darkness of the wood on to a small lane running gently downhill.

The moon was still high and bright and not far ahead of us we could see cottages on the right-hand side of the lane.

'Where are we?' I asked.

'If my recollection of the Ordnance Survey sheet is accurate,' he replied, 'we are at the edge of the hamlet of Buckstone, beyond which lies our destination.'

I cast a glance back at the woods.

'They cannot be very far behind us, Holmes,' I said.

'They will await the recovery of their priest or whatever he may be,' said Holmes, 'and he will send them after West. West is far more important than we are.'

'How is that?' I asked.

'Because we have only seen what we have seen, but West knows what he knows.'

'Do you think that they will catch him?'

He shook his head. 'I should not think so. He took his opportunity and ran like a man possessed. He was well away before any of them had the wit to chase after. Unless he does something stupid, he will have made good his escape.'

'Then we have only ourselves to consider,' I said. I looked around me once more. 'It is not the best of landscapes,' I said.

'Why not?' he asked.

'If I understand the situation,' I said, 'there are two usual routes from here to Weston Stacey—by this lane and by the footpath across the Mayfield. They are bound to look for us on both.' I looked around us at the moonlit landscape. A slight breeze had risen, driving waves through the standing wheat and giving the fields the appearance of a monochrome ocean.

'With this moonlight,' I said, 'and not a trace of cloud coming up, we cannot make across open country. They would spot us in an instant.'

Holmes smiled. 'Then,' he said, 'we shall have to take a leaf out of your own book, Watson. Have you forgotten how you and Colonel Harden escaped from Moriarty's roughs in Herefordshire seven years ago?'

Recollection dawned on me and I protested. 'Holmes!' I said. 'That was by way of a ditch! Surely you are not suggesting that we crawl from here to the village through the ditches?'

He laughed. 'Good old Watson!' he said. 'I believe you would attempt it if I suggested it, but you need not fear. Pass me your necktie if you will.' It crossed my mind to wonder at his request, but I was too exhausted to pursue the point. Quickly I dragged my tie from my collar and passed it to him. He stooped and selected a largish pebble from the ground and proceeded to wrap my necktie about the stone. Stepping back along the lane, as coolly as a bowler measuring his run, he turned, took two or three quick paces forward and flung the wrapped pebble along the lane with the skill and grace of a Test player. Then, pulling his own necktie loose, he repeated the process. The two ties lay in a patch of moonlight in front of the hamlet's cottages, tiny spots of colour in the eerie grey and black landscape.

Holmes cocked an ear. 'I think,' he said, 'that I hear sounds of pursuit,' and with a quick movement he slid noiselessly into the bushes at the edge of the lane.

I too could now hear the distant shouts of our pursuers moving through the wood and I lost no time in following my friend into the bushes. Beyond them I found Holmes seated on the bank of a small stream, removing his boots.

'Come, Watson!' he urged. 'The hunt is up. Off with your boots and stockings and we shall go home by water.'

I followed his instructions, but I was less than confident of his plan.

'Will this stream really take us back to the village?' I asked. 'And can we walk the whole way? What if it deepens or has holes in its bed?'

'Again,' he said, 'the Ordnance Survey has revealed to me that this water flows right through Weston Stacey and most conveniently it skirts the rear garden of the John Barleycorn, taking us right to our door. As to risk, I am surprised that a man raised in the country does not recognise that watercress is taken from this stream and that plant only thrives on shallow, flat gravel beds. I do not think we need to fear stepping into a hole.'

'But what of our neckties?' I grumbled, as I rolled up my trouser-legs and slung my boots about my neck like a schoolboy.

'That was merely to mislead our pursuers into believing that we have fled by road, flinging away our restricting haberdashery as we went.'

He stepped into the water and I followed. Together we paced slowly and as quietly as we might along the bed of the little brook. I soon realised that Holmes was right and that we could walk with tolerable ease on the level gravel.

We had not gone far when we heard voices in the lane as the pursuing party arrived. Holmes drew me to a halt and we stood silent, the brook rippling about our bare ankles, and listened to the discovery of our neckties and the excitement that ensued. With enthusiastic cries the pursuit took off along the road to Weston Stacey.

'If you have a cigarette about you, Watson,' said Holmes, 'I think we might now enjoy one without risk.'

So, paddling like otter-hunters or school-children, we made our way slowly along the shaded bed of the stream until it opened out alongside the garden of our lodgings. There we sat on the bank, restored our footgear and made ourselves as respectable as we might

135

before entering the inn's back door.

Our landlord was still up and came out of his parlour with a lamp in hand.

'Good evening, gentlemen,' he greeted us. 'I hope you enjoyed your exercise.'

'Oh, indeed,' retorted Holmes. 'It is a magnificently moonlit night and we have thoroughly enjoyed a bracing walk.'

15

THE MORNING AFTER

It may be imagined that my injuries of that night did not make me an early riser next day. Indeed, hardly had my head touched the pillow, it seemed, than a cheerful chambermaid was bringing me hot water.

The bruising of my throat had eased somewhat with rest, but my stomach muscles ached abominably and it was minutes before I could force myself out of bed and stand at the wash-stand. When I had shaved and dressed I made my way cautiously downstairs, fully expecting to be before Holmes, and was the more surprised to find him seated at the breakfast table with a pot of tea before him.

'Good morning, Watson,' he said. 'I deemed it unfair to start without you, but if you will press the bell our host has been ready to serve for some minutes.'

I was not at all sure that I required much by way of breakfast, but I pressed the bell as suggested and lowered myself warily into a chair at the table while my friend poured me a cup of tea.

The landlord appeared within seconds bearing a loaded tray, and the odours of hot food rapidly restored my appetite.

As he served us our host asked, 'Was you up by Buckstone Wood last night, by any chance, gentlemen?'

'No,' said Holmes, promptly. 'Our stroll took us in the other direction entirely.'

'Well then, you missed a fine old set-to at Buckstone Wood.'

'Really?' said Holmes. 'What has been happening there?'

'Well, it seems some of the village lads was of the same mind as yourselves, to enjoy the moonlight last night. They was up about Buckstone Wood and they ran into a band of poachers and there was a rare old battle. These poachers had guns, of course, and poor old Charlie Bates got himself shot in the arm.'

'With a shotgun, one imagines,' said Holmes with a glance at me.

'No, sir. They had pistols, these poachers, and it were a pistol bullet that they put into Charlie. Dr Ryall was up half the night, fixing him up, and one or two others as was bruised.'

'There was a substantial band of poachers,

then?' asked Holmes.

'Oh yes, sir. They reckons there was about five or six of them, terrible big fellows. They comes out from Swindon, you know, from the railway works, and poaches roundabout here.'

'And where was Sergeant Bullington while all this was going on?' said Holmes.

'Well, of course, he didn't know nothing about it while it was happening like. Nobody knowed anything about it till they come back to the village and woke up Dr Ryall.'

'One had hoped,' said Holmes, 'that a little place like Weston Stacey might be more peaceful than London, but perhaps we were wrong.'

'I don't know what things are coming to,' said the landlord. 'What with a little child being murdered in our fields and poachers fighting with guns in the woods, you're right, sir, it ain't safe at all,' and clucking censoriously he left us.

'Half a dozen large, armed poachers, eh, Watson?' said Holmes, with a thin smile. 'At least it will serve to maintain our innocence of any involvement.'

I was relieved to hear that our part in the night's events seemed to be unrecognised, but my head was full of questions that I wanted to ask Holmes and, over our food, I began.

'That mumbo-jumbo last night, in the wood,' I said. 'What on earth was going on? It looked like something out of the Middle

Ages.'

He smiled. 'So it may be, Watson. So it may be. It is certainly something of great age.'

'Well, are we dealing with black magic, or what?'

'I wish it were so simple,' he said. 'We have run across that peculiar delusion before, but this is something new to me.'

'But what on earth is it? That ceremony or whatever it was last night was purely blasphemous.'

He laughed. 'If people choose to worship in peculiar ways that is their affair, Watson. It is only when their worship involves the slaughter of innocent children that it becomes a matter of public concern.'

'Then the ceremony and the murders are linked?'

'Indubitably,' he said.

'Then what is going on?'

'I cannot be entirely sure,' he said, 'and at first I was unwilling to believe the evidence, but last night's events have confirmed some of my deductions in this matter.'

I was still confused and my expression must have shown it, for he went on.

'We began,' he said, 'with one unsolved murder of a little girl. We are agreed that she was not killed for gain nor, most probably, for revenge. The manner of her killing ruled out perverted lust. In addition, we know that more than one person was involved.'

'How do we know that?' I asked.

'Watson!' he snapped. 'This all began because PC Russell heard a vagrant confessing to what seems to have been knowledge of or involvement in the death of Beatrice Collins. Sergeant Bullington was anxious to suppress that confession.'

'Yes,' I agreed

'Then it stands to reason that the vagrant and Sergeant Bullington had some shared guilty knowledge, does it not?'

'I suppose so,' I said.

'Dear me, Watson. Last night's exploits seem to have left you considerably less than your usual self this morning.'

There was no disagreeing with that, so I offered no reply.

'Plainly the little girl's death was the work of a group,' he continued, 'but I was hard put to it to see what manner of group might benefit in what way by the death of an innocent labourer's child. Such indications as there were led me to considerations which, at first, I was inclined to reject, inasmuch as they seemed in the highest degree unlikely.'

I was about to interject, but he carried on.

'Nevertheless,' he said, 'those indications were very singular and were confirmed when our investigations in Berkshire revealed a repeat of the patterns.'

'To what patterns do you refer?' I asked.

He shook his head. 'Watson, how often have

I remarked to you that the accumulation of data is a meaningless enterprise unless it can be made to reveal significant patterns?'

'True,' I admitted. 'But I do not see—'

He interrupted me again. 'We have already rehearsed the similarities between the manner in which Bea Collins and the Berkshire lad died, even to the traces of sugar at the scenes.'

'I have been wondering about the sugar,' I said.

'So you may, Watson. So you may. But I shall return to the sugar in a moment. Have you not understood the significance of the time and place of each killing?'

I thought for a moment. 'Each was killed on their way home at the end of a harvest—the haymaking in Berkshire, the corn harvest here,' I said.

'Well done!' he exclaimed. 'You are returning to life! But what else? What of the places?'

'Each was killed in a field,' I said.

'But not just any field, Watson. What were the names of the fields?'

'Why, the Mayfield here and—what was it?—the Fair Meadow in Berkshire.'

'Exactly!' he said.

'But how does that assist us?' I asked.

'Because, Watson, it is evident that both children were killed at a specific time and in a specific place. Each was slain as a harvest was ending and each was slain in a place that

141

enjoys, or in the past had enjoyed, a certain significance to the local populace. The Mayfield can only have got such a name because it was anciently the place where the villagers held their May Day ceremonials. The Fair Meadow will have been named because it was once the site of some ancient fair or revel. The map of England is covered in such names—Midsummer Hills, Fair Greens, Summer Lanes—which memorialise the older ceremonies of our fathers.'

'But why at the conclusion of the harvest?' I asked.

'You have heard Constable Russell tell of the "crying of the neck",' he said. 'When does that occur and what is its meaning?'

'He said it occurred when the last sheaf of the last field was cut, and the neck was preserved until the next harvest.'

'Exactly so, Watson! It is a survival of a pagan observance, the purpose of which, as one harvest ends, is to ensure continuity and prosperity—to guarantee a good harvest in the next year. So is the stump of last year's Yule Log used to light the Christmas fire—to ensure continuity and prosperity, Watson—mankind's most ancient longings.'

The light dawned. 'Then these poor children have been slaughtered like sacrificial animals to guarantee a good hay or corn harvest next year!' I exclaimed.

'Precisely so,' he said.

I sat, stunned. If he had explained his conclusions before I had witnessed that grotesque and evil ceremony at the Buckstone, I do not think I would have believed him but now the pieces slid into place and I realised that some grisly association of maniacs was slaughtering the children of the poor in the belief that their foul crimes would bring down blessings on their community.

'But this is monstrous, Holmes. These fiends are slaughtering children with no more compunction than you or I would kill a rat!'

'They have been, Watson, but I assure you that they will do so no more.'

It was on the tip of my tongue to ask him about the significance of the sugar, when the door opened to admit the landlord.

'I do beg your pardons, gentlemen,' he said, 'but Constable Russell is outside and asked if he could speak to you on a matter of urgency.'

My heart missed a beat as I considered the possibility that our friend had come to arrest us for the shooting of Charlie Bates, but Holmes smiled affably.

'If you will be good enough to supply us with more tea and an extra cup and saucer, you may show the constable in,' he said.

Our host was back in minutes with a fresh pot of tea and accompanied by the young policeman. Russell's face was pale and worried.

Holmes motioned him to a chair and poured him a cup of tea. 'Now, Constable,' he said, 'what brings you here this morning?'

'It's Sergeant Bullington, gentlemen. He didn't arrive for duty this morning, which is the first time I can recall, so I went along to his house to see if he was unwell. He's dead, Mr Holmes. Stretched on his hall floor, dead.'

16

THE SCENT OF MURDER

'Dead!' we exclaimed simultaneously, and even in my surprise I was aware of a most peculiar expression flitting across my friend's face.

'Like I say,' the young constable said, 'he's laying on his hall floor dead.'

'When did his death occur?' asked Holmes.

'I can't say, sir.'

'Then when was he last seen alive, Constable?'

'He was at the station when I reported for duty last evening, sir, and he went his round of the village before signing off.'

Holmes nodded. 'So he did. We saw him at the John Barleycorn. Our landlord tells us there was some kind of disturbance last night and people were injured. Was the sergeant involved in that, by any chance?'

Russell shook his head. 'If you mean the fight over in Buckstone Wood, no, sir. We knew nothing of that till this morning. Dr Ryall

144

come in and says as he'd treated Charlie Bates for a firearm injury and various others for bruises and that. I sent Constable Wilkes to obtain a statement from Bates.'

'You did not think to inform Sergeant Bullington?'

'Not at that point, sir, no. You see, the poachers were long gone. I thought it more important to have all the evidence available for the sergeant when he came on duty, but the probationer come back and the sergeant hadn't turned up.'

'What did you do then, Constable?'

'Well, I thought the sergeant must have been taken poorly, because he's never late on his turn, so I thought I'd pop along to his house and see what was the state of things.'

'And what did you find?'

'I knocked at his door and waited but there wasn't any answer, so I knocked again. There was still no answer, so I tried the door. It wasn't locked, so I went in, calling out for Sergeant Bullington as I went. That was when I found him, Mr Holmes. He was sprawled on the hall floor in his dressing-gown and pyjamas.'

'And you are sure that he is dead?'

'I wasn't at first, of course, but I looked and saw his eyes was open and fixed. Then I searched for a pulse like they train us to do, but I couldn't find none and there was no trace of breathing, so I was certain he was dead.'

'Evidently you suspect foul play,' said

Holmes. 'May I ask why?'

'His face, sir. He is bruised about the face as though he had been in a bad fight.'

'I see,' said Holmes, and that strange expression flickered on his features once more. 'I take it that you have not disturbed the body?'

'Oh, no, sir. I left everything just as it was and came straight here, Mr Holmes.'

'Very good,' said my friend. 'Then we had best finish our tea and come with you,' and suiting the action to the word he drained his cup and rose.

The sergeant's house was at the far end of the village close to the police station but we were there in a short time.

PC Russell pushed the front door open and Holmes stepped to the entrance and looked in, motioning us to keep back. For minutes he crouched beside the sprawled body, his eyes sweeping the area, his long fingers occasionally touching the body or its surroundings. Then he leant back on his haunches and called us in.

Sergeant Bullington lay face down with his head towards the front door. His head was turned to his left and his left arm doubled under the body while his right arm was extended and partly bent. He was clad in striped pyjamas and a nondescript blue dressing-gown and shod in worn red leather slippers. The left side of his face was grazed and reddened by small abrasions, though the general complexion was unnaturally pale. The body partly concealed a small pool of vomit on the hall rug.

Holmes nodded towards the corpse. 'What do you make of it, Watson?'

I knelt and examined the dead man. When I turned his head carefully I could see that, apart from the minor contusions on the left side of the face, there was a very large bruised area on the right side, centred about the right eye-socket.

'He has certainly been involved in a fight,' I confirmed, 'and very recently, for the discoloration of his injuries had only begun and was not complete when he died. It is a hot morning, so it is difficult to judge when he died, but from the state of *rigor mortis*, I would say no more than five or six hours ago and possibly a lot less.'

'And what killed him?' asked Holmes.

'It is conceivable that the blow to his right eye, which seems to have been a severe one, may have caused injury to the brain,' I said. 'The brain,' I explained for Russell's benefit, 'can be jarred inside the cranium, can bounce as it were, in response to a severe blow. When that happens it can be injured by impact with the interior of the skull. When that occurs it is what we call concussion, but it may cause death.'

I looked again at the body.

'The vomiting,' I said, 'might indicate

147

concussion.'

'Then you believe he died from the delayed effects of a blow to the head?' asked Holmes.

I shook my head. 'I cannot say that,' I said. 'My first impression is that such a cause is possible. It might, equally, be some failure of the heart or it could be a stroke, though he seems to have been a hardy and fit man. I do not believe I can offer a reasonable opinion without further information.'

'Very wise,' said my friend. 'Then we must seek further information.'

He straightened up and all three of us stepped cautiously around the body to the rear of the little hallway. On the left a half-open door gave entry to the front sitting-room and Holmes entered.

The little room was well furnished and heavily carpeted. In the bay window a small table supported an arrangement of wax fruit surmounted by two colourful stuffed birds, the whole under a glass dome. Before the fireplace were two heavy wing-backed armchairs, between which stood an occasional table formed from a large disc of beaten brass, incised with patterns and coloured here and there with red, green and blue enamel, supported on a six-legged frame of black-enamelled wood. On its top lay a papier-mâché tray, enamelled in black and bearing a Japanese decoration in white and vermilion, and on the tray stood a black-glazed teapot, decorated with white and blue flowers and two cups and saucers, both seemingly Chinese in design. Beside the tray was an earthenware tobacco jar.

The walls of the room were hung with framed photographs, mainly of Sergeant Bullington in army uniform or police dress with one or more colleagues. Larger than the others, a hand-carved wooden frame held a studio portrait of a handsome Indian woman of about thirty years, her head covered by a shawl and a jewel gleaming in her nostril.

Holmes sniffed the air.

'Do you detect an odd scent, Watson?' he asked.

I sniffed. 'I cannot say that I do. There is a slight odour of pipe tobacco, but I cannot detect more.'

'No matter,' he said. 'You have been in Sergeant Bullington's home before?' he asked of PC Russell.

'Yes, sir.'

'And have you taken tea with him?'

'On occasions, yes, sir.'

'In this room?'

The young constable shook his head. 'No, sir. Always in the kitchen, Mr Holmes.'

'And not, I'll wager, from porcelain Chinese teacups,' said Holmes.

'No, sir. Normally from a plain mug, sir.'

'Then we know that the sergeant had a visitor last night, and we also know that he regarded that person as his social equal, if not his superior,' said Holmes. 'What is more, since we know where the sergeant was after he finished his duties, and we know that he was involved there some little time, then it can only have been at a very late hour when his visitor arrived.'

Both Russell and I looked surprised.

'Excuse me, Mr Holmes,' said the policeman, 'but how do we know where he was and what he was doing after he left the police station?'

Holmes made no answer, but stepped into the hall and reached into the umbrella stand, lifting from it the sergeant's silver-headed staff. He held it between his hands as he re-entered the room.

'You will recall, Watson, that at the Buckstone last night I found myself embroiled with a tall man in a black cowl?'

'You was at the Buckstone last night, Mr Holmes?' asked Constable Russell.

Holmes stopped the young man with an imperious lift of the hand. 'You will also recall,' he continued, 'that the same person attacked me with a staff and that I fended off his blows with my swordstick?'

I nodded and he rolled the staff between his hands. Half-way along it could be seen a fresh mark, where a fragment of its stained wood had been sliced away.

'Taking this mark,' said Holmes, 'together

with the injuries to Sergeant Bullington's face, have you now any doubt that the sergeant was the man who conducted that blasphemous ceremony at the Buckstone last night and the man with whom I fought as we escaped?'

'None whatever,' I said, 'but—'

He lifted his hand again. 'Perhaps it would assist if you were to describe to Constable Russell what really happened in Buckstone Wood last night, and identify to him the half-dozen poachers from Swindon who caused such mayhem to the village labourers. In the meantime, I shall search for the further data which we require.'

He went off up the stairs and PC Russell and I took the two armchairs. The constable got out his notebook.

'I'm not sure,' I said, 'but I think it would probably be better if you heard what I have to say and made no note until you have spoken further with Holmes.'

'Very well, sir,' said the constable and slipped his notebook back into his pocket. 'Perhaps you will explain to me how you and Mr Holmes came to be in Buckstone Wood last night and what really happened there.'

Choosing my words carefully, I described how we had been at the John Barleycorn when the man West had arrived in a state of alarm, believing that he was the object of the Devil's attention. I told how his words had alarmed his fellow labourers and how Holmes had deduced that some kind of meeting was about to take place at the Buckstone.

Choose as I might, I had no adequate words to describe my reaction to the grotesque and sinister ceremony that we had witnessed at the Buckstone, nor the chill that had run through me when, after they had taken their vote, that solo voice had chanted the beginning of the old drinking song in the darkness of that reeking glade:

'There were three men came out of the West, their fortune for to try,
And these three men swore a solemn oath John Barleycorn should die.'

I must have managed to make some sense of my strange narrative, for PC Russell interrupted me not once while I described the whole of the night's events—our firing on the group, West's escape, our running battle and finally our strange road home.

When I had finished the young officer sat silent for a moment, as though trying to absorb it all.

'You believe that West was being sentenced to death, as it were, Doctor?'

'I cannot understand any other meaning in what they were about,' I said, 'and certainly he was in a state of abject terror until we interrupted.'

'But who were this group of people? You

152

say they was all labourers from the village?'

'With the exception of the cowled man, the priest or whatever he was, the rest of the group were all men that I have seen in the John Barleycorn. I now agree with Holmes, that the robed and hooded man must have been Sergeant Bullington.'

He shook his head. 'But what is this, Doctor? You make it sound like the Devil's work indeed.'

'In my experience,' said Holmes from the doorway, 'the Devil is semi-retired. It is some long time since he carried out his own dirty work. Nowadays he leaves it in the hands of evil and stupid human beings who can be entirely trusted to do his work for him.'

He stepped into the sitting-room and held up a long black robe with a hood.

'I found this in the late Sergeant Bullington's wardrobe,' he said. 'Which, I believe, clinches my identification of him as my attacker last night. I found also further evidence of whatever it was that killed the sergeant.'

'Really?' I said.

He nodded. 'The evidence indicates that he had retired to bed when he was seized by sickness. Evidently he left his bed to seek a remedy or summon assistance. He vomited twice more, once on the landing and once more on the hall rug as you saw. What do you make of that, Watson?'

I was perplexed. 'It does not,' I said, 'sound

like either concussion or heart failure. If I were pressed I would have to say that it seems like some form of poisoning.'

'Poison!' exclaimed Constable Russell.

'Poison,' said Holmes steadily. 'Let me essay a few conjectures. It is always an error to theorise without data, but I believe that we have sufficient facts to draw a few reasonable inferences.'

He held out one hand and struck off his points as he made them with the index finger of the other.

'First,' he said, 'West is frightened by a freak of nature into believing that the Devil is seeking him out as a result of some wickedness in which he and his fellows have taken part. Secondly, his appearance at the inn and his wild language so frighten his comrades that they feel he is unreliable and may betray them. Accordingly they call a meeting of their conspiracy to deal with West. Thirdly, the officiating priest, or call him what you will, at their ceremony is Sergeant Bullington and a vote is taken that West shall die.'

He paused and the recollection of the previous night made me shudder again.

'At that point,' continued my friend, 'Watson and I took a hand in their proceedings, allowing West to make good his escape. The meeting broke up in confusion and we managed to escape without being identified.'

'But what of the other person, or whatever

it was?' I asked. 'The thing that emerged from behind the Buckstone?'

Holmes laughed, shortly. 'Billy Hayter's monster, you mean, Watson. It was nothing more than a tall person in fancy dress, decorated with a few skulls purloined from Mr Trentham's ossuary, much as the Lord of the Manor used to appear at Witches' Sabbaths clad as the Devil. However, in that person lies the crux of the case and the heart of the conspiracy. This has not all been constructed by a policeman and a bunch of farm labourers, gentlemen. Whoever it is that played the monster last night is the progenitor of this madness.'

He paused again. 'What is more,' he continued, 'is it not a reasonable inference that, after the disruption of their ceremony and the escapes of West and ourselves, Sergeant Bullington and that person met here, late last night, to consider the position they were in?'

We nodded, dumbly.

'And is it not equally reasonable that the same person believed that the sergeant had compromised himself and, like West, had best be eliminated?'

'But what can I tell my superiors, Mr Holmes?' asked Russell.

'You may tell them what you know, Constable,' said Holmes, 'and let them take me up for having caused an injury to Sergeant Bullington which brought about his death and arrest Watson for shooting Charlie Bates.'

'But I cannot do that, Mr Holmes. It is not what I believe.'

'I am glad to hear it,' said my friend. 'In that case, you had better let me destroy this robe and take samples from the teacups, after which you should report to your superiors the entirely mysterious demise of Sergeant Bullington and leave them to solve it if they can. You might also enquire, discreetly, into the whereabouts of poor West.'

17

A SUMMONS TO THE MANOR

Holmes found a small phial in the sergeant's kitchen which enabled him to secure a sample of the dregs of tea from the cups. He was careful enough to take a pinch of the tobacco from the jar on the sitting-room table as well.

As we made our way back to the inn, I asked, 'What will you do now?'

'This changes very little,' he said. 'It is useful to have confirmation that Sergeant Bullington was deeply involved in this affair, but we suspected as much from the first and, after struggling with him last night, I was quite sure.'

'It is a pity,' I suggested, 'that he has not survived for you to confront him.'

'That is, of course, precisely why he was eliminated, but it makes little difference. I would not have confronted him in any case.'

'Why not?' I asked.

'Because a crooked police officer is the worst kind of villain when it comes to extracting a confession. Either they remain obstinately silent, relying on the difficulties of obtaining proof, or they use their skill and knowledge of the law to raise complicated structures of lies and half-truths that are the very Devil to unravel.'

'Then what will you do?' I asked again.

'I shall have to return to London,' he said, 'if only briefly. I need my microscope and my chemical apparatus to examine the samples which I have taken this morning. In addition there are certain matters which I must look into which can only be done in London. I only hope that I can do so without drawing the attention of my brother to my presence in the capital. I had hoped that this matter might keep me at a safe distance until His Majesty's Coronation was over.'

'Holmes,' I said, 'what is it about Mycroft that makes you so anxious to avoid him at the moment?'

'My brother,' he replied, 'as I have already told you, has conceived the notion that the new King should award me an honour.'

'Yes,' I said, 'but you told me that you had refused.'

'So I have, Watson, so I have, but my wretched brother—who will, of course, receive a knighthood himself as the expected reward of his service on retirement—is deeply desirous that I should be similarly rewarded for those occasions when he has called me in to assist in some official matter. So he will not take no for an answer and continues to importune me to accept. His Majesty's illness and the cancellation of the Coronation has merely given Mycroft additional opportunities to importune me on the subject. Really, I believe that I shall not be safe from his ambitions until Edward is seated in the Abbey with his crown firmly on his head.'

'But would it be so very bad to accept?' I asked.

'In short—yes. Oh, I know you will point out that I have accepted honours from other nations, and so I have, but to accept one in my own country is entirely different. When I am called in by foreign countries or their royal families I am merely a consultant, as one might employ a French chef or a German piano-tuner. I feel fully entitled to accept rewards offered for my services. In Britain I cannot avoid a certain old-fashioned feeling that I have a duty of loyalty to the Crown and to the nation and that to make a profit or to accept an honour for my efforts would cheapen the relationship. In addition, I have said to you on occasions that I sometimes believe that I am the last Court of Appeal in England. If I am to remain so, it must be seen clearly by anyone who might seek my assistance that I am entirely independent of any official mechanism. No, Watson, no matter how much it would please brother Mycroft, firmly intend to remain plain Mr Sherlock Holmes.'

There was evidently nothing more to be said on the matter, and we completed our stroll in silence. Back at the John Barleycorn we found our host in a fine state of excitement. Rumour had reached him of the death of Sergeant Bullington, and he and his regulars were alike agog. Having seen us leave with PC Russell, he imagined that we were privy to all official secrets and sought to extract them by artless questions.

'I knew young Constable Russell was upset when he come for you gentlemen this morning,' he remarked. 'I imagine that would have been in connection with the sergeant's going off?'

'It was merely,' said Holmes, 'out of consideration for Dr Ryall, who had been up half the night, treating the injured from the Buckstone Wood affray, that PC Russell recalled that my friend is a doctor and asked him to examine the sergeant.'

'He is definitely dead, then?'

'Oh, yes,' I confirmed. 'He is definitely dead.'

'And what might be the cause, if I might

make so bold?' he enquired.

I shook my head as convincingly as I could. 'PC Russell merely asked me to confirm the fact of death,' I said. 'No doubt the county police will have a more detailed examination made by Dr Ryall or some other police surgeon.'

'Do you think it might have had something to do with them poachers up in Buckstone Wood as I told you about?' he asked.

'I should think not,' I said. 'As I understand it, Sergeant Bullington was not involved in the affray in Buckstone Wood.'

'No, that's right, he wasn't,' said the landlord. 'Still, it's an awful thing, gentlemen. It makes you think, don't it?'

'It does, indeed, make one think,' said Holmes. 'Perhaps we might have our luncheon now, landlord?'

Our host hurried away to do his bidding, still shaking his head at the vagaries of fate, and was back very shortly to begin serving us. He brought with him an envelope and handed it to Holmes.

'I had forgot, gentlemen,' he said, 'and I do apologise, but all this with the sergeant drove it clean out of my head.'

He handed the letter to Holmes, who opened it, glanced at the contents and passed the letter to me. It was a single sheet of crested notepaper, heavily embossed, and it bore the address, 'The Manor, Weston Stacey, Wiltshire' and that day's date. The note beneath the heading read:

Gentlemen,
My brother and I understand that you are taking a holiday in Weston Stacey and would be pleased if you would join us for tea this afternoon and perhaps an inspection of our collection of tropical plants.

Yours sincerely,
George and Henry Devaux.

I looked and whistled softly under my breath.

'The Devaux brothers!' I exclaimed. 'Lords of the Manor! What can they want with us?'

'We have made ourselves a curiosity, Watson, by our intrusion into the countryside and, as such, the Devaux brothers wish to cxaminc us.'

'Shall we go?' I asked.

'Why not, Watson? Why not? My curiosity is fully as great as that of the Devaux brothers.'

'You think that we may acquire further data?'

'I do not see why not. The Devaux brothers, like Sergeant Bullington, like Platt, like Miss Thorne, have strong Indian connections and the Indian element in our mystery is the most powerful and singular part of it.'

The landlord, when he knew of our

161

appointment at the Manor, was all for lending us his trap and stable-boy to deliver us in style; but it was a fine day and, after a shave and a change of linen, we set out on foot.

Weston Manor stood a little way out of the village on a gentle slope and, as we approached, the road curved around the outside of the Devaux estate. A solid brick wall marched alongside us over which hung the branches of fine trees, both deciduous and coniferous, and some of which I could not identify.

At length we came to the gateway, an imposing arrangement, flanked by pillars topped with heraldic gryphons, where an elderly gatekeeper came out of his lodge and swung open the wide, wrought-iron gates that protected the entrance. Before us stretched a long, curving driveway, bordered by long-established stands of rhododendrons, so that the house itself was invisible from the gates.

We had made our way perhaps half-way up the drive, and still not caught a glimpse of the house, when we heard the sound of hooves and wheels on the gravel ahead and saw Miss Thorne, accompanied by her uncle's groom, approaching us in the vicar's trap.

'Good afternoon, gentlemen!' she called as we raised our hats, and motioned to her groom to stop.

'I understood that the Devauxs had invited you,' she said, as we stepped across to the trap.

'I have been taking advantage of their generosity to take some of their wonderful flowers.' She motioned to an enormous bunch of sumptuous blossoms that lay in the rear of the trap. 'Uncle's garden is past its best in high summer, but there is always something wonderful in the Manor hothouses. I am sure you will enjoy seeing them. There is really nothing like them, except perhaps at Kew.'

'We look forward to it,' I assured her.

'I have, for professional reasons, made some study of oriental and tropical plants,' said Holmes, 'and I'm sure an inspection of Mr Devaux's collection will prove rewarding.'

We tipped our hats again as she went on her way and we continued towards the house. Of a sudden in rounding a bend in the drive, the house was in front of us. I do not recall what I had expected, but it was not the large, ornate but relatively modern house that stood before us. Built in red brick, plentifully relieved and decorated with bands and facings of white Portland stone, it reminded me of nothing so much as the great hospital at Netley where I had studied medicine for the Army.

We stood under the porch and rang the bell, which was answered promptly by a white-uniformed and turbanned khitmugar. He ushered us into an enormous entrance hall, dark and cool despite the hot, sunlit afternoon. As he hurried away to his masters, we looked about us.

The floor beneath our feet was richly carpeted in the finest and most decorative of Eastern carpets, though here and there it could be seen that beneath them lay a marquetry surface, elaborately patterned in many exotic woods. Rich and colourful oriental hangings shrouded the walls lit by small lamps in coloured glasses.

As our gaze travelled round the room I felt my heart thump at one point. At the far end of the hall, standing in a niche obviously created for it, was a great dark statue. For a moment, in the gloom I had seen the very image of the grotesque thing that had writhed in front of the Buckstone on the previous night.

We stepped towards it and I could now see that it was a figure, modelled larger than lifesize, in dark bronze. It depicted a female of striking beauty but most ferocious aspect, poised on one leg as though dancing and with arms outstretched. A coronet girded her brow and a long skirt of ribbons or grasses depended from her waist while around her shapely neck hung a necklace of human skulls.

'Good afternoon, Mr Holmes, Dr Watson,' said a voice behind us. 'I see you are admiring my Bhowanee, my Kali.'

18

THE CORPSE FLOWER

'You are well informed, sir,' said Holmes, turning to meet the newcomer. 'May I ask if I am addressing Mr Henry Devaux?'

'You are, sir.' Devaux was a tall man in his middle years, perhaps a shade taller than Holmes, and broad with it. He was dressed in a cream linen soft-collared shirt, worn under a cream flannel waistcoat decorated with fine embroidery, together with cream flannels. A pair of direct grey-blue eyes looked out of a round, fresh-complexioned face and a thick moustache swept from side to side of his jowls.

'Then I, Mr Devaux, am Sherlock Holmes, and this is my friend and colleague, Dr Watson. May I ask how you knew our identities?'

'No secret about that, gentlemen. Cecily Thorne told us. Mind you, she said you were operating incognito and all that. Swore us both to secrecy, so you've no need to worry.'

He stepped forward and shook hands with both of us. 'I am delighted,' he said, 'to make your acquaintance, gentlemen, but I confess that I wonder what brings you to a sleepy little place like Weston Stacey.'

'That is simple,' said Holmes. 'I am here

because the brutal slaying of an innocent child has passed unsolved for a twelve-month.'

'Ah yes,' said Devaux. 'The affair of the little Collins girl. That was very bad. I sit as a JP, you know, for this Division. There's nobody on our bench, not even the oldest, who recalls anything quite like it.' He shook his head. 'A very nasty affair indeed.'

'Do you think the county police were sufficiently active in the matter?' asked Holmes.

'Sergeant Bullington did his best, I suppose, and he had additional officers for a little while, but they couldn't make sense of it. I suppose you know that the sergeant died last night? Miss Thorne was just telling us.'

Holmes nodded. 'I was aware of the fact,' he said. 'PC Russell asked Dr Watson to examine the body. He seems to have died of some form of heart failure.'

'Really?' said Devaux. 'I would have thought him too fit for that. Mind you when I first knew him he was a heavy drinker.'

'You knew him for some time?'

'Oh, indeed. The Devaux headquarters in India is at Tokot, and when I was a youngster in the company office Bullington was a sergeant-major in the garrison there. He got into quite a lot of hot water, nearly lost his rank over his drinking escapades, but Miss Thorne's parents were alive then. They ran the local mission. They straightened him out and moderated his drinking. That and his woman.'

'His woman?' queried Holmes.

'It was well known in Tokot that Bullington was living with an Indian woman in the town. Of course, if he hadn't been a senior NCO he couldn't have got away with it. Perhaps that slowed his drinking down as well.'

'Is it not somewhat strange,' said Holmes, 'that here in this little village there is a small congregation of persons who knew each other in various capacities in India?'

'Not really,' said Devaux. 'Teddy Trentham came here because I have the gift of the living of this parish and I put him in, because I'd known Cecily and her parents in India. Bullington kept in touch when he came home, and when he was looking for a quieter billet than Liverpool I said a word to the Chief Constable here.'

'And Mr Platt?'

Devaux laughed. 'Our Harvest Lord? Well, he's an old Devaux employee, you know. Went out as a boy and was a clerk in the offices, then he was put in charge of labour on our plantations. Same sort of thing as Bullington. When he wanted to come home, we suggested that he get into the harvest gang business and we'd recommend him to all the farmers on the estate. Of course, we don't force them, they can hire who they like, but old Platt seems to suit most of them well enough.'

Holmes had turned his gaze once more to

the bronze statue. 'Kali, I believe?' he said.

'That's right,' said Devaux, 'Kali or Bhowanee or Devi. Nice piece of work, but an unprepossessing lady, don't you think? We found her in the ground, near Tokot, when we were digging a railway siding, and my young brother brought her home. Looks well enough there, but Teddy Trentham won't let the choir come into the hall to sing carols at Christmas, makes them stand outside. Says it's not right to sing Christian hymns in front of a pagan idol of death.'

'She is, I believe, a Hindu fertility goddess? A sort of Demeter or Astarte?' suggested Holmes.

'That's it,' said Devaux, 'but she was also the Number One goddess of the Thugs, you know, a goddess of death.'

'But surely,' I said, 'the Thugs were not Hindus.'

'No, Doctor,' he agreed. 'Thuggee was a separate cult but somehow they adopted Kali as their goddess. In fact Thugs belonged to other faiths—they were Mohammedans, Sikhs, Hindus, what you will—but they also practised Thuggee. It was a sort of professional faith.'

'A professional faith?' I queried.

'Yes,' he said. 'They believed that spiritual merit was achieved by robbing and killing so they waylaid travellers, killed them with their rumal, buried their bodies and went on their way convinced that they had done their mistress's wish.'

'Rumal?' I asked.

'It's a handkerchief, or neck-cloth,' he explained.

'Why did they kill with the rumal?' asked Holmes.

'Their legends said that Kali here was once attacked by a demon. She fought back and spilled his blood, but every drop of blood that fell turned into another demon and attacked her. She called upon the Creator who told her to kill the demons without shedding their blood, so she strangled them. So her followers were enjoined to kill by strangulation wherever possible. They carried the rumal in their dhotis—their loincloths—with a corner sticking out. The thing was weighted with a coin tied in one end and they could whip it around someone's neck and apply pressure in an instant.'

'The street bandits of Hell's Kitchen in New York have a similar technique,' remarked Holmes. 'There they take a dead rat, stuff it with lead shot and tie a string to its tail. One of them stands at the mouth of an alley with his colleagues hidden behind him. He whirls the rat on the string, for all the world simply a disgusting child with an unpleasant plaything. If a well-dressed man passes by, the urchin will whip the weighted string around his throat and pull him to the ground, where the gang falls upon him, chokes him, loots his pockets and

169

vanishes into the slums.'

My blood ran cold at my friend's calm dissertation on methods of choking and I shuddered at the recollection of the grip on my own throat in Buckstone Wood.

'But the Thugs are gone?' said Holmes. 'They no longer exist?'

'Oh no,' replied Devaux. 'Sleeman put them down in the twenties of the last century. He rounded up thousands of them, got some of them to turn informer and broke the whole thing up. Many of them were hanged and a lot were transported. They wouldn't have lasted long, in any case.'

'Why not?' said Holmes.

'Civilisation,' said Devaux, 'the coming of the railway. Once wealthy travellers began to cross India by train the Thugs would have been out of business, you see. They couldn't operate on the railways the way they could on country roads.' He tapped the bronze goddess familiarly. 'I imagine that they buried her when Sleeman got after them. Thought it would all blow over and they could come back for her one day, I dare say.'

'But they no longer exist?' Holmes persisted.

Devaux shook his head. 'I've never heard of them anywhere in India these days. We thought it might be starting again a few years ago. We had a number of murders of children around Tokot all at once, but that wasn't

Thuggee. Turned out they were killed by their parents or sold to be killed, to bring someone good luck. We were on that pretty sharp and it soon died out. No, Thuggee's gone, Mr Holmes. Devauxs have interests from the Himalayas to Ceylon, but we never ran across them in my time. I suppose there might be a few old faithfuls left. You can't really stamp out a secret society unless you know you've exterminated them all, but I've never heard of any recent outbreak. If you want to know about Thugs, you should have met Grandpa. He was with Sleeman when they rounded them up.'

He gazed at the figure of Kali again. 'But I'm forgetting my duties,' he said. 'Here I am jawing away about Thuggee and I dare say you're both gasping for a drink.'

'The discussion of any aspect of crime is always a fascinating topic to me,' said Holmes, 'but I'm sure we would welcome a sample of Devaux's famous tea.'

Our host led us through a drawing-room as dark and cool as the hall and filled with objects of Indian craft, and through french windows on to a terrace at the rear of the house. A table stood there surrounded by basket chairs. Devaux showed us to chairs then called for a servant. The same white-clothed manservant who had admitted us appeared.

'Ali,' said Devaux, 'we will have tea now, and ask Mr George if he feels well enough to join us.'

While we awaited service I looked around. Below the veranda a flight of shallow stone steps led down on to a wide lawn which swept away down a slight slope and ended in a stand of colourful trees whose foliage was unfamiliar to me. Along the left-hand side of the lawn, and at a level with the veranda, stood a long glass hothouse, like a miniature version of the Crystal Palace, though it was large enough in itself.

Devaux saw my interest in the building.

'That's brother George's province,' he said. 'Ever since he returned from India he's collected trees and shrubs and flowers from India and what won't grow outside he brings up in that glasshouse. Mind you, they say he's got as fine a collection as Kew in there. I don't know, I'm not a flowers man.'

'What brought you both back from India?' asked Holmes.

'Duty,' said Devaux. 'We have a system in the family. Some of us have got to run the business out there, some of us have got to run the estate here. We have two brothers out there, and my two sons, but it was time for me and George to come home largely because of his health.'

'His health?' I took up.

Devaux nodded. 'India's not a place that suits everybody. It never bothered me. I'm the sort of fellow who makes himself easy anywhere, but George had a lot of trouble with his health and in the end the doctors said he must come home or India would kill him. He took it very hard. He loved the place—fully intended to end his days there. Since he came back he's done nothing but study, Indian flowers and trees, Indian history, Indian art, Indian religion. He's made a little India here at the Manor.'

From behind us a thin voice quoted, " 'Once you've heard the East a-calling, you can never heed aught else." '

We turned to see what must be Mr George Devaux stepping cautiously through the french windows, assisted by a silver-headed cane. He was, I suppose, taller yet than his brother, though his stoop made it difficult to estimate. His face was lean and lined, coloured with that grey-yellow tinge that is often the mark of tropical infections, and his eyes were obscured by blue-tinted spectacles. He wore a long, exotically patterned, satin dressing-gown and, despite the warm day, a silk scarf wrapped tightly around his throat.

He laid his stick against the wall and lowered himself carefully into a chair. Once he was seated, the manservant brought tea, sandwiches and cakes.

'Once we have refreshed ourselves,' he said, in that same thin, high, voice, 'I hope you will let me show you our hothouses. Are you interested in plants, Mr Holmes?'

'My interest is a little specialised,' he replied.

'I know those plants which produce poisonous alkaloids.'

The younger Devaux laughed. 'Then you must definitely see my collection, Mr Holmes, for I have many of that kind. I even have a plant from the East Indies which the natives call the "corpse flower". They say that it eats people.'

'Really?' said Holmes. 'I had thought your collection was exclusively Indian.'

'Devauxs,' said the invalid. 'are thought of in England as the suppliers of widely known brands of tea, but our interests in the East are wider. We grow not only tea, but rice, millet, maize, indigo and rubber. Our plantations are spread throughout India from the Himalayas to Ceylon, but are also in Burma, the Malay States and the East Indies. While my health permitted me I travelled in all those areas. Now I have to recreate them as best I can in my hothouses.'

'On the way up your drive,' said Holmes, 'I marked your fine stands of rhododendrons. Do you not have difficulty in persuading them to grow on this chalky soil?'

'You are more knowledgeable about plants than you admit, Mr Holmes. Yes, they are difficult to start. They prefer a solid, rocky environment, but once started they quickly spread and acidulate the soil.'

The conversation turned away from plants. We chatted about the harvest prospects. Henry Devaux assured us that the reaping was well under way on the outer farms.

'Unless the weather breaks, old Platt will soon have his gang at Toadneck Farm and we can have our Feast and settle down for the autumn. At least, once Cecily's had her Coronation Festivities. She's been pestering us for weeks to lend this and pay for that. Her parents were the same in Tokot—thought every last beggar in the town was their responsibility, and Cecily's the same. Can't say if the labourers are grateful for what she does for them, but she looks after them morning, noon and night. Sometimes I think I'm wasting my time as Lord of the Manor. Cecily's got the welfare of the place well in hand.'

Tea over, George Devaux lifted himself with difficulty from his chair, took up his stick and led us along the veranda to where a walkway connected with the near end of the huge hothouse. He unlocked a door and stood aside as we stepped into his domain.

Two things struck me immediately on entering the building. One was the moist heat of the atmosphere, the other the rich burden of variegated scents carried on the hot, wet air. From my distant recollections of India a quarter of a century before, I was prepared to acknowledge that George Devaux had indeed recreated that land in his great glasshouse.

For more than an hour we walked behind him as he showed us the beautiful and exotic flowers, shrubs and even large trees which he

175

had nurtured there. Finally, when we had walked almost the length of the building, he brought us to a plain door and extracted a key from his dressing-gown pocket.

'You wished to see my prize plant, Mr Holmes,' he remarked. 'There!' and he flung the door wide and stepped back.

I followed Holmes into the last section of the hothouse. This time the air was not heavy with sweetness. It was as hot and moist, but foul with the ripe scent of death and decay. For a moment I believed that some large animal had died among the foliage and rotted in the wet heat. My eyes watered at the filthy stench and it was only when I had wiped them dry that I was able to see our host's pride.

In front of us stood the most bizarre plant I have ever seen. A tall, tapering spike of a pale, lemonish tint stood several feet high, higher in any case than Holmes' head, emerging from a deep fringed circlet formed by a single folded petal. Where the central spike was pale and almost colourless, this petal from which it sprang was a rich, deep maroon in its interior and a completely different colour on the outside, a vivid, almost turquoise, green.

Holmes stood rapt, while I gagged at the appalling smell of the thing.

'There,' said the younger Devaux, 'is the East Indian corpse flower, Mr Holmes. Is it not wonderful?'

'*Amorphophallus gigantum*,' said Holmes, in

176

a tone of genuine admiration, 'and you must have nurtured it with great skill to bring it to such a size and into flower. Even the one at Kew has only flowered twice since they had it.'

Devaux smiled at the praise. 'Thank you,' he said. 'Of course, it does not really eat people. It feeds upon insects, rather like our own little sundew, but one can see why its dreadful odour made the natives believe that it was a corpse-eater.'

'Oh, indeed,' said Holmes. 'I am really most grateful to you for the opportunity to see it in flower. I was unable to view the Kew specimen in flower and have only seen illustrations.'

The older Devaux had wisely remained outside the chamber.

'Would anyone,' he enquired, 'care for a long brandy and soda? It might remove the taste and smell of my brother's infernal daffodil.'

'It is not,' said his brother, 'a daffodil, Henry. It is rather a lily, a cousin of our own Easter lily, but I expect our guests would appreciate a brandy.'

I should record that, in the event, it took a number of brandy and sodas to eclipse the appalling smell of that bizarre lily.

19

IN THE WORKHOUSE

'What,' I asked Holmes as we made our way back to the John Barleycorn, 'do you make of the Devaux brothers? Apart from anything else, they barely look like brothers, only in their height.'

'The same, Watson, might be said of myself and Mycroft. As to what I make of them, Henry Devaux is a quite unsurprising man who has devoted himself to the affairs of the family company and now equally devotes himself to the affairs of the estate. You will find his like—retired military men or men of affairs— all over England, successfully filling their retirement.'

'And the younger brother?' I asked.

'Bizarre as he seems at first sight, he also conforms to a type, a fact which he recognised with his introductory quote from Kipling. There are certain Englishmen who seem to flourish in the East as they have, never bloomed at home, and who seem to find in the Orient what they have never found in England. I would not say it is necessarily a bad thing— after all, their number includes some of our most adventurous explorers, our most imaginative military men and our most able administrators. If they really cannot develop their potential at home, it is probably best that they flower abroad and do the Empire credit thereby.'

'Then you do not find him strange?' I asked.

'I did not say so, Watson. I said that he, like his brother, conforms to a recognisable type, but it is, you will agree, a strange type. Would you say that "Chinese" Gordon or Sir Richard Burton or Raja Brooke were ordinary men? Would you not have categorised them as "strange"?'

'Well, yes,' I said 'but they pursued their involvement with the East abroad.'

'And George Devaux, through the accidents of illness, has been unable to do so. Had his health stood up he would no doubt still be in that country, and no requirement of the Devaux business interest would have brought him back to England for long. As it is, a man who had embraced India is forced to live out his days in England and makes that more palatable by attempting to re-create India in miniature about him. I do not find that strange.'

'And you do not suspect him in connection with the murders?'

'Watson, you have known me long enough to know that from the outset of an enquiry I suspect everyone, apart from you and me, until the accumulated data or my inferences therefrom eliminate them. That being my invariable method, I suspect George Devaux—but no more than I suspect his brother Henry.'

In the bar of the John Barleycorn that night the labourers seemed subdued and there was no singing, though whether this was because of their tiredness after a long day in the fields or because of Sergeant Bullington's death we could not determine. Shortly before closing PC Russell made the round of the bar and paused by our table before he left.

'Good evening, gentlemen,' he said.

'Tell me,' said Holmes, 'what have your superiors made of the sergeant's death?'

'Very little,' said the constable. 'They seem to be satisfied with the view that the sergeant was taken ill in the night and came downstairs, in the course of which he tripped and fell, injuring his face and bringing about his death.'

Holmes snorted quietly. 'Then it would be as well to leave them in their ignorance,' he said. 'Though I shall still take my samples to London and see what the test-tube and the microscope may reveal. Have you been able to discover what has happened to West?'

'No, sir,' said Russell. 'He lives in lodgings with old Mrs Shallow but she hasn't seen him since the night before last. She says that after he was brought home from here, unwell, she saw him to bed. Then, later that night, three of his workmates called for him and he went with them. She hasn't seen hide nor hair of him since and all his belongings are still at her cottage.'

'So,' said Holmes, 'if they have not caught and killed him—and I do not believe they have—he has had the wit to put some distance between himself and his former colleagues. Which is a pity, because I would dearly like to have a word with Mr West. He knows clearly enough now that he has nothing to gain by keeping silent, that the only real protection is to tell all that he knows and let us bring this thing to an end.'

'So you still intend to go back to London?' I asked, when Russell had gone.

'Only for a day or two,' said my friend. 'You can stay here and hold the fort for me.'

Now I was always in two minds when these situations arose. On the one hand I was deeply pleased that he honoured me with his trust in looking after his investigations in his absence, but on the other hand I was uncomfortably aware that, no matter how I tried to apply his methods and sought to determine what Holmes would do in any situation, I always seemed to fall short of his expectations and, if he did not tell me so directly, he certainly let me feel it.

'What do you require me to do?' I asked.

'Firstly, to keep in touch with Constable Russell and look for further news of West.'

'What if he is dead?'

'He is not dead,' asserted Holmes.

'You have said so before,' I agreed, 'but I admit I do not entirely agree with you,

Holmes.'

'It is not merely that he put a good distance between himself and his pursuers at the Buckstone, Watson. It is the evidence of a late meeting at Sergeant Bullington's home.'

'I don't follow you,' I said.

'Sergeant Bullington played his part in the ceremony at the Buckstone until we interrupted it. Then he fought with me, not knowing who I was. West fled and some of them pursued him but they returned empty-handed. Sergeant Bullington went home and had a meeting with someone. What must have been the topic which they discussed, Watson?'

'Why, the danger to which they were exposed—West having evaded their death sentence and strangers having seen their ceremony and both having got away.'

'Precisely, Watson. Now, I have remarked before that West was by far the greater danger because he could tell what he knew, and he knew something that frightened him of hellfire. For all Bullington or his visitor knew, we might really have been poachers who stumbled upon them by accident and, having escaped, would bring them no harm.'

'But who was the visitor, Holmes?'

'My next point,' he said. 'Whoever it was, they held rank in this bizarre organisation, for they executed Bullington without any ceremony. And they did so to prevent Bullington panicking and talking of what he knew. With

West at large they are all in danger and the sergeant might have decided to change sides so he was eliminated.'

'Then you believe that the sergeant's visitor was the person in charge of this disgusting cult?'

'Indubitably, Watson, for they acted immediately and with their own authority to silence Bullington. Their next move must be to seek out West and kill him—but in such a way that his colleagues know that the organisation's vengeance has been effected. That has not occurred, or we should know about it. *Ergo*, unless he has done away with himself, he is not dead, and the more time that passes without his body coming to light the more convinced I am that he is alive and can lead us to our prey.'

'But if he is dead—or if we cannot locate him?' I asked.

Then we must fall back on my deductions as to the purpose, time and place of these killings and wait for the next attempt. That will take place when the neck has been cried in a few days' time.'

'So, if we cannot find West or otherwise identify the master of this conspiracy, we must let another child run the risk of murder?'

'I fear so, Watson. I see no other way.'

My mind ran back more than twenty years, to the day when I had first heard of Holmes from my old friend Stamford. Stamford had found Holmes too scientific—approaching cold-bloodedness. I recalled his words, 'I could imagine his giving a friend a little pinch of the latest vegetable alkaloid, not out of malevolence, you understand, but simply out of a spirit of enquiry in order to have an accurate idea of the effects.' I hoped very earnestly that Holmes would identify the killer before the harvest's end; I was deeply unhappy with the alternative—of leaving one of those hapless labouring children exposed as a lure to the killer. It smacked of cold blood, of the goat tethered under a tree to lure a tiger in front of the hunters' guns, and it could go dreadfully wrong.

Nevertheless, I also recalled that Stamford had said that to do Holmes justice, he believed that Holmes would take a pinch of poison himself with the same readiness. I knew that, if he were forced to adopt his second approach to the mystery, he would spare no effort to preserve the life of the child in question and would, indeed, gladly sacrifice his own to protect it. Still, I hoped that West would soon turn up and would be willing to tell us all.

On the following morning I accompanied Holmes to the railway station, where he caught a mid-morning train to London, reminding me that I could always use the telephone at the village post office to contact him at Baker Street.

I walked back from the station deep in thought. It was evidently of the greatest importance that West be found and interviewed before his fellows could lay their murderous hands on him. I considered how I could assist Holmes in that respect, but it seemed to me that all I could do was to keep my eyes and ears open about Weston Stacey and maintain contact with Constable Russell.

The thought had barely crossed my mind when Russell hove into view on a bicycle, pedalling hard towards the station. Seeing me he swung himself down from his machine.

'Good morning, Doctor,' he called as he crossed the road. 'I was told at the John Barleycorn that Mr Holmes was leaving for London and I had hoped to catch him before he left.'

'There has been a development?' I asked.

'There has indeed,' he said. 'West has turned up. He's in the workhouse at Swindon.'

'Splendid!' I exclaimed. 'I shall take my luncheon, then go over to Swindon and see what I can make of him. Will you come with me?'

He shook his head. 'I cannot do that,' he said. 'There's only me and the probationer here, now, you see, so I've got to keep hereabouts. Still, sure you shan't need my help, Doctor.'

I was excited by the opportunity that chance had presented to do something which would materially advance Holmes' enquiry and, at the same time, avert the dangerous possibilities inherent in his alternative scheme. I hurried over my meal and was soon on my way back to the little station.

On my way I met Miss Thorne. 'I hear that Mr Holmes is gone to London,' she said. 'Are you off to join him?'

'No, no,' I replied. 'He has gone for a day or two, but he will be back. I have a little business in Swindon to which I must attend.'

'Then I must not keep you from your train,' she said, and whipped up her pony.

It was not difficult to locate the workhouse once I had arrived at Swindon. I presented myself to a bespectacled clerk in a little office at the door, gave him my card and asked if I might see the new entrant, West.

He looked at my card thoughtfully, then looked up at me over his glasses. 'What did you say your business was with this West, Doctor?' he asked.

I had not stated my business but saw no harm in telling the truth. 'I have been staying in the inn at Weston Stacey, which is West's home. I happened to be present when he had a kind of seizure the other day and I treated him. This morning the village constable told me that West was in your care, so I thought I'd look in and see if there was anything I might do for him.'

He nodded. 'I see, Doctor. Perhaps you'll be kind enough to take a seat in the little room over there. I shall be back in just a moment.'

He indicated a small, glass-panelled room across the lobby, I followed his pointing finger and took a seat on a hard wooden bench while the clerk went off in search, I imagined, of West.

His moment had been considerably extended when I heard the fall of hard boots on the floor of the lobby and looked up, expecting to see West. Instead I saw the clerk returning with a slender man in civilian clothes and two uniformed police officers, a sergeant and a constable.

He opened the door of the waiting-room and pointed to me. 'That's the man,' he said to the civilian, who I now realised must be a detective officer, and he pressed my card into the detective's hand and went hurriedly back to his desk.

The detective stepped into the room, followed by his two colleagues. The constable shut the door behind them and all three of them stood, the detective foremost, looking at me in silence.

'May I ask,' I demanded, 'what is going on here?'

'You may,' said the detective. 'I am Detective Inspector Hamblin of the Wiltshire police. You, according to your card, are Dr Watson of 221b Baker Street, London. Is that right?'

'It is,' I said. 'I am the associate of Mr Sherlock Holmes, the consulting detective.'

The inspector smiled, an unpleasantly thin and sardonic smile. 'So you're the colleague of the great Sherlock Holmes,' he said.

'That's right,' I said, and he interrupted me before I could continue.

'If you are the Dr Watson that writes the stories about Mr Holmes,' he said, 'you will be well aware of his habit of criticising the official police and pouring sarcasm on their methods.'

I was becoming distinctly uneasy about my situation and I saw no benefit in answering his remark. 'My address is on the card,' I said. 'If you have any doubt as to my identity, you may telephone Mr Holmes at that address,' and I recited the number.

He nodded. 'And of course,' he said, 'most of England knows Mr Holmes' address from your stories, Doctor. It remains to be seen as to whether that telephone number is genuine, but they are easy enough to get hold of.'

'I suggest you telephone him straightaway,' I said, 'and, in the meantime, you might explain to me what my visit here has to do with the police.'

'I,' he said, 'have been called here to investigate what may well be a murder. You— Doctor—may have something to do with it. Consequently, I am arresting you on suspicion in connection with the murder of Samuel West. Put the darbies on him, lads, and bring him along to the station.'

20

THE INTERROGATION OF A SUSPECT

In more than twenty years of association with Sherlock Holmes I had found myself in many strange and dangerous situations. More than once I had been his accomplice in crime, often I had come within a hair's breadth of death or serious injury and on numerous occasions I had been made to feel completely ridiculous. On one occasion I had even passed the night on the floor of a madman's padded cell, wrapped in a canvas strait-jacket. All of these things I had suffered willingly, as part of the price of my friendship with a uniquely talented man who claimed no other friend in the world. Nevertheless, my mood when I was frog-marched through the streets of Swindon and flung unceremoniously into a police cell was not one of resignation.

I raged inwardly at Holmes, for departing and leaving me in Weston Stacey when an important development was likely to occur; I raged at myself for being so anxious to figure in Holmes' good books that I had not waited until he returned. I raged at the sardonic Detective Inspector Hamblin, who appeared to me far worse than the most oafish of the Scotland Yarders, and promised myself an accounting with that gentleman when my *bona fides* was established.

In the end my anger ran itself dry, and I began, more calmly to assess my situation. Freed from the handcuffs, I had been placed in a twelve foot by six foot cell, containing only a brick bed shelf, topped with wooden slats and supplied with one thin, stained blanket, and a malodorous galvanised pail. At the back of the cell a single, high, barred window admitted a small amount of light. I deposited myself on the uncomfortable bed and began to wonder.

West was dead, apparently murdered, yet only that morning PC Russell had said that he was in the Swindon workhouse, so it seemed that he had died during that day. Of the manner of West's death Hamblin had given me not a hint, and I was hard put to it to understand how the avenging hand of the conspiracy at Weston Stacey had reached into the workhouse walls and executed him. I was also aware that, had I travelled to Swindon as soon as I knew West's whereabouts, I might have prevented his murder and enabled Holmes to acquire useful information from the man. Of one thing I was certain—that West had, indeed, been murdered. If I have learned nothing else from my association with Sherlock Holmes, I have acquired his deep suspicion of anything that appears coincidental.

This train of thought also ended nowhere and eventually I fell into an exhausted doze.

My personal property had been taken from my pockets on arrival at the police station, so that I did not know how long I had been asleep when I was awakened by my cell door banging open.

A young constable stood in the doorway with an enamelled mug of tea. 'When you have drunk that,' he said, 'Inspector Hamblin would like a word with you.'

He stood by while I gulped down the lukewarm, sweet tea then escorted me along a passage to a room where Hamblin and his uniformed sergeant sat at a table. Hamblin motioned me to a chair as the young constable closed the door on us.

'Now, Doctor,' he said, 'I hope you are suitably refreshed and in a more co-operative frame of mind.'

'A more co-operative frame of mind!' I exclaimed. 'I was going about my legitimate affairs when you accused me of murder and had me flung into a cell. Is that likely to make me co-operative?'

'Your legitimate affairs,' he said. 'Let me tell you a little story, Doctor. Then we'll see how legitimate your affairs may be.'

He unbuttoned his waistcoat and leaned back in his chair, his thumbs in the beckets of the waistcoat.

'Yesterday,' he said, 'the village constable at Weston Stacey telegraphed a notice that a man named Samuel West was missing from his

191

lodgings in that village and there was reason to suppose he might seek to harm himself. Late last evening the said Samuel West was taken into custody outside a public house in Regent Street here, where he had been causing a disturbance by urging peculiar religious ideas upon a group of railway workers.'

'That is not in the least surprising,' I said. 'Two days ago West had an unfortunate experience. He was struck by some kind of minor whirlwind while crossing a field near Weston Stacey. I saw him and treated him immediately afterwards and it was evident that the poor man had interpreted a natural phenomenon as a personal attack on him by the Devil. It seems to have turned his wits, for he left his lodgings that night and did not return home.'

Hamblin nodded. 'So far we can agree, Doctor, that West was raving. When he was brought here it was soon obvious that there was no sense to be got out of him. For that reason it was decided to lodge him in the workhouse for the time being. As a doctor— that's if you *are* a doctor—I'm sure you know that sometimes these people calm down overnight and give nobody any more trouble. We thought we'd leave him there to cool down, and alert the county asylum in case he got no better and we had to take him there.'

I nodded. 'He was certainly very disturbed when I saw him two days ago. But that was immediately after the incident with the whirlwind or whatever it was.'

'Was he now? And that was because of a whirlwind? Perhaps you'd better tell us about it, Doctor.'

I explained that I had been holidaying at Weston Stacey and detailed the circumstances in which I had treated West. 'I came to know,' I concluded, 'that he was in the workhouse here and I dropped by to see if I could be of any further assistance.'

Hamblin nodded. 'So Samuel West was driven out of his mind by some kind of whirlwind which he thought was the Devil?' he said.

'That's right,' I agreed.

'Oh no, Doctor. That's not right at all. When Samuel West was arrested in Regent Street, he was imploring a bunch of lads from the railway works to pray for him. He didn't say as the Devil was after him, Doctor. He kept saying as there was a deadly female after him, who would kill him if she got the chance.'

I realised at once that the poor madman had been referring to Kali. In his distorted brain he believed he was her creature and that, having been accused of betraying her, she would destroy him. I saw no way of explaining that to the inspector, so I held my tongue.

'But that isn't all, Doctor. As I say, he was taken to the workhouse, where he was given a strong sleeping draught, but he kept the whole place awake with his ravings. The night clerk became suspicious that there was something more than madness in West's ranting. He says that West kept saying that he had let murder be done and now he would be murdered.'

Once again I stayed silent. Hamblin eyed me for some time before going on.

'So we come to this morning,' he said, at last. 'When the night clerk came off duty, he told the workhouse master about Samuel West's ravings and the master told him to report the matter here, which he did. I was about to go across to the workhouse and see if I could make any sense of it all, when we had another message from the workhouse master, to the effect that Samuel West was dead and the workhouse nurse believed as he'd been poisoned.'

He dropped his chair back to the vertical with a bang, and leaned across the table. 'Now, Doctor, if you really are the man who writes the Sherlock Holmes stories in the *Strand,* I'm sure you'll know that Mr Holmes does not believe in coincidence, and there, for once, the official police agree with him. So when I heard that a man who said that he was going to be murdered had died suddenly, perhaps by poison, I thought that to be beyond coincidence and I went straightaway to the workhouse.'

He paused again and I felt the need to say something. I had the feeling that remaining silent only served to increase the inspector's suspicion of me.

'Look here,' I said, 'I've told you how I came into contact with West. Now if he has met his death in some strange way, whether by someone else's hand or not, I'm sorry, but I still fail to see what you believe connects me with his death.'

Hamblin raised a hand. 'Bear with me, Doctor. We have as much time as we need, and I wouldn't want to leave anything out, or to get things in the wrong order. At eight o'clock this morning West had his breakfast along with the other inmates. It seems he ate heartily and was a bit quieter than he had been. After breakfast he was separated from the other paupers and put in a quiet room. They do not assign lunatic paupers to the workshops because of the disruption they cause.'

He leaned even further forward. 'Now,' he said, 'we come to what may be the nub of the case. At some time during this morning a little parcel was left for West on the clerk's desk in the lobby. Nobody saw who put it there, as the clerk was obeying a call of nature at the time. It was a little bundle wrapped in brown paper. The clerk saw that it was marked for West and opened it, to see that it didn't contain any forbidden matter like alcohol. In fact, he says it contained only a little tin of boiled sweets, a bar of Fry's chocolate and a twist of coarse tobacco. He saw no harm in West having those

195

items and they were given to him. When he was called for dinner, he was dizzy and pale. He couldn't eat his dinner and was taken with diarrhoea and vomiting. The workhouse matron saw him. What was it she said, Sergeant?'

He turned to the sergeant, who had been taking notes. That officer turned back several pages of his notebook and read aloud, ' "He was pale and sweating. He complained of dizziness and shortness of breath. He vomited several times, bringing up blood, and he seemed to have no control of his bowels. I suspected that he had eaten something that disagreed with him and gave him an emetic. He vomited again, but it did not lessen the symptoms. After an hour and a half he collapsed in a faint and never recovered." '

'Thank you, Sergeant. Now, does that sound like poisoning to you, Doctor?'

'I have to agree that it might well be,' I said.

'Exactly,' said Hamblin. 'You have to agree. Well now, Doctor, consider this. Samuel West goes into the workhouse last night, ranting about being murdered. This morning an anonymous party delivers a seemingly innocent package for West and shortly after that the man dies, apparently of poisoning. What would Mr Sherlock Holmes make of that, Doctor?'

'I admit that you have good grounds for suspicion. Have the contents of the parcel been examined?'

'Oh, yes, Doctor. He had eaten the chocolate and some of the sweets and they are being analysed at this very minute.'

'It certainly seems possible that he was poisoned,' I said.

He nodded. 'But then what happens?' he asked. 'Hardly has West breathed his last but a mysterious doctor turns up at the workhouse.'

'There is nothing mysterious about that at all,' I interjected. 'I have explained my presence there.'

'So you have, Doctor, so you have. But there are one or two things you have not explained. For example, I have wired the landlord of the John Barleycorn at Weston Stacey. He does not recall a Sherlock Holmes and Dr Watson staying there, but he does recall a Mr Sigerson and a Dr Wilson. Now, what do you make of that?'

'I can only imagine that the stupid man has made some kind of mistake,' I said, but even in my own ears the answer sounded unconvincing.

Hamblin drew a pocketbook from the inside of his coat and I realised that it was my own. He extracted two cards and laid them on the table.

'Now, the landlord might have made a mistake, Doctor, but here coincidence raises its ugly head again. He recalled a Dr Wilson and here I have two business cards, both of them found in your pocketbook. One says you are Dr John H. Watson, MD, of 221b Baker

Street, London. The other says you are Dr James H. Wilson of 338 Marylebone Road, London.'

He looked at me, levelly. I had no answer to give that was not going to make the situation much worse. Holmes with his usual attention to detail had provided us with cards supporting our assumed identities.

'And who better,' he asked, 'to know about poisons, than a doctor, whether you're Dr Watson or Dr Wilson or Dr Whoever? Eh?'

I was in an entirely false situation from which I could not extract myself. Holmes would never forgive me if I told the entire truth and, if I did, Hamblin would never believe me. If I continued to tell less than all of the truth, the question of my double identity cast doubt on anything which I said. I recollected that attack is the best mode of defence and summoned my indignation.

'I have told you,' I declared, 'that I am Dr John Watson, the friend and associate of Mr Sherlock Holmes. I have given you the number of his telephone. If you place a call to him, I am sure that he will confirm my identity. Beyond that, I have nothing further to say to you!'

'It might interest you to know, Doctor, that I have placed a call to Mr Holmes. His landlady tells me that he is away from London, somewhere in the West Country she believes, and she does not know when to expect him.'

He smiled, triumphantly, that same thin smirk. I had reckoned without Holmes' desire to avoid his brother. No doubt he had told Mrs Hudson that all messages that were not from me were to be given a false explanation.

There was one slender straw which might restore my credibility, though I hesitated to use it.

'In that case,' I snapped, with as much confidence as I could muster, 'I suggest that you call Inspector Lestrade at Scotland Yard. Until you do so I shall still have nothing to say to you.'

He drew out his watch and looked at it. 'Inspector Lestrade,' he said, 'if he is sensible will not be at the Yard. I shall call him in the morning. In the meantime, you may cool your heels and consider whether you wish to co-operate. Take him away, Sergeant!'

21

THE POISON TREE

If I was restless when first incarcerated, I was a hundred times more so at the prospect of being kept in custody while Hamblin pursued his theories. Through a sleepless night I tossed on the hard plank bed, turning over and over in my mind the steps by which I had been placed in a totally false position. No matter how I considered the problem, there were no answers I could now give which would satisfy Hamblin's suspicion of me. I had to leave everything in the hands of Lestrade.

It had been light for hours and my cell was already uncomfortably warm when the door banged open and a constable appeared.

'Come with me!' he commanded, and led me through the corridors again to a small office, not the room where I had been questioned on the previous evening.

Hamblin sat at a desk smoking a cigarette. A tattered copy of the *Strand Magazine* lay in front of him.

'Good morning, Dr Wilson, or is it Watson? There's someone on the telephone who wishes to hear your voice,' and he nodded to an instrument on the wall behind him, the earpiece of which had been placed on top of the box, not on the rest provided.

My heart leapt, for I thought that it might be Holmes. I crossed the room in two steps and snatched up the earpiece.

'Hello,' I said. 'This is Dr Watson. Who is calling?'

There was a thin chuckle at the other end of the line and a voice said, 'This is Inspector Lestrade, Doctor. My colleague down there says you have got into a spot of bother.'

I silently damned Lestrade for a clown. 'Look here,' I said, 'Inspector Hamblin is concerned about my identity.'

'He's concerned about more than that, so far as I can make out,' said Lestrade. 'He seems to think you're a poisoner, Doctor.'

I began to protest, but Lestrade interrupted me. 'Now, now,' he said. 'I've explained to my colleague that if you are indeed Mr Holmes' partner then he can strike you off his list of suspects.'

'But of course I am,' I said.

'Well, you'll have to forgive me, Doctor, but voices always sound so different on these confounded machines. Everybody sounds the same, like a rat down a drain. Now, can you tell me something that'll prove your identity to me?'

'What sort of thing?' I asked, growing more exasperated.

'Well, something that an impostor would be unlikely to know. I know—how about your middle name? There's not many people know that, I'll wager.'

He was right. Having spent a part of my boyhood at an English school I had soon learnt that the possession of a Gaelic middle name was not something to advertise.

'My name,' I said, as clearly as I could, 'is John Hamish Watson.'

'Then it is you, Doctor,' he said. 'Put me back on to Hamblin, will you, Doctor?'

I handed the earpiece to the inspector, who exchanged a few words with Lestrade then hung up. Sitting again, he opened the copy of the *Strand* and looked me up and down.

'Your friend Lestrade suggested that I compare you with the pictures in this,' he said. 'But I have to say that the illustrator seems to have done you rather more than justice.'

'Some people have managed to recognise me from those illustrations,' I said. 'Perhaps Paget never saw me after I'd spent a sleepless night in one of your infernal cells.'

'Shouldn't go about pretending to be who you aren't,' he said, unruffled. 'Now, if I was you I'd get my property back from the duty sergeant and go away.'

'And that's all?' I said.

'If you were looking for an apology, Doctor, you'll look for a long time. If Lestrade hadn't vouched for you, I had a bad time planned for you. After all, any friend of Sherlock Holmes is no friend of mine.' Saying which, he lobbed the magazine into the waste-paper basket.

I did not wait for a second dismissal. Moments later I was at the duty sergeant's desk recovering my property. He eyed me up and down as he laid the items out.

'You didn't enjoy our hospitality then, Doctor?' he said.

'No,' I said. 'Nor did I enjoy the ridiculous suspicions of your detective inspector.'

He smiled under his moustache. 'Well, he's known for being a sarcastic man at the best of times, and this morning he's particularly

202

narked.'

'Narked?' I queried.

'Yes, sir. He thought he had a nice little murder case and a suspect in custody all on one day, and now it's all gone pear-shaped.'

'You mean in having to let me go?' I asked.

'Well, that's a part of it, but the other's worse. They telephoned from the laboratories twenty minutes ago. They couldn't find any poison in the sweets or the chocolate, so the inspector hasn't got a murder let alone a suspect.'

I don't know whether I was the more pleased at Hamblin's discomfiture or outraged that, knowing he had no case, he had put me through that humiliating charade with Lestrade. I bade the sergeant a good morning and left. Hurrying through the streets of Swindon I was acutely aware of my last appearance in the town. I could not shake off the feeling that every bystander or passer-by was someone who had seen me frog-marched in handcuffs on the previous afternoon.

It was not until I was safe in the privacy of a railway compartment that my composure returned and I set out to order the events of the past twenty-four hours in my mind. Then it struck me like a blow in the face. On one point I was entirely in agreement with the odious Inspector Hamblin—that West's death was most unlikely to be a coincidence. Yet there was no poison in the gifts left for him!

I churned this puzzle about in my mind all the way to Weston Stacey, but was no nearer a solution on arrival. At the John Barleycorn the landlord welcomed me effusively.

'There was a message,' he said, 'from the Swindon police, by prepaid telegram, as they wanted to know about a Dr Watson staying here. I told them your name was Wilson, sir. I hope I did right.'

'Absolutely,' I said. 'It was a silly mistake. I got involved with a fatal accident in Swindon and the police needed to check, but they must have written the name very badly. Can you have the maid arrange a bath for me?'

I made my way to my bedroom and, in a few minutes, the chambermaid tapped my door to tell me that a bath was waiting in the dressing-room between my room and my friend's.

I wallowed long and luxuriously in the warm, soapy water, anxious to scrub or soak away every trace of Swindon police station. While I did so I was pleased to hear Holmes' key in the lock of his bedroom and water splashing into his wash-basin. I dried myself, summoned the boy to remove the bath, and went into my room to change.

I emerged a few minutes later feeling a good deal better than I had been. There was silence from Holmes' room, but I knew he would have heard my vigorous ablutions and would appear when he was ready so I settled myself into a chair and picked up the unread newspaper that I had brought from Swindon, noting as I did so that a fresh jar of tobacco stood on the table. It was my favourite Arcadia mixture and I blessed Holmes' thoughtfulness in having brought me a fresh supply from London.

Minutes later Holmes joined me smiling broadly.

'Good day, Watson!' he said. 'Do I understand that you have been in difficulties in Swindon?'

'How on earth did you come to hear of it?' I demanded.

'Lestrade,' he said, 'met me at Paddington as I was boarding the express. He thought it a huge joke.'

'Well, I do not,' I said. 'What is more, the serious part of the affair is that West is dead.'

'Is he indeed?' said Holmes, and fell into a chair. 'I think you had better tell me all about your trip to Swindon.'

In as much detail as I could recall, I gave him the story of events from the point where I had met PC Russell. He sat with his head thrown back, his eyes closed and his fingertips steepled before him during my narrative.

When I had done he opened his eyes and leaned forward. 'You did well,' he said, somewhat to my surprise. 'But it is indeed unfortunate that West has been murdered.'

'Then you believe he was murdered?' I said.

'What else, Watson, what else? It is in the

highest degree unlikely that he would die coincidentally at a time when he had fled from the murderous clutches of his fellows. No, there I must agree with your Inspector Hamblin.'

'But there was no poison found in the chocolate or the sweets,' I argued.

'Then,' said my friend, 'it would seem likely that he was poisoned by the same mechanism that destroyed Sergeant Bullington.'

'Ah!' I exclaimed. 'So Bullington was poisoned? You must tell me how you confirmed the suspicion.'

I leaned forward, taking my pipe from my pocket, and reached for the jar of Arcadia mixture. Holmes sprang from his chair and his right arm shot out, hitting my hand and sending the jar tumbling. I fell back into my chair, utterly bewildered.

'Holmes!' I cried. 'What in Heaven's name are you doing?'

'You shall see, Watson. In the meantime, if you require tobacco, please make free with mine,' and he passed his pouch across.

'You asked,' he said, when I had filled my pipe with his rough-cut shag and got it going, 'how I confirmed that Bullington was poisoned. You will recall that I took samples of the dregs of tea left in the cups on his table.'

I nodded and he continued. 'Those specimens revealed no trace of poison.'

'Then how was he poisoned?' I asked.

He drew a white envelope and his lens from his pocket. 'I have remarked often enough, Watson, that once one has exhausted the impossible, whatever remains, however improbable, must be the truth.'

'But there was only tea on the table,' I objected.

'Not so, Watson,' he said, and laid the opened envelope on the table, shaking a number of small fragments of something out on to the flap. 'Look there,' he said and passed me his lens.

'It is tobacco' I said, without recourse to the lens. 'The tobacco was poisoned!'

He nodded. 'Use the lens,' he said.

I peered closely at the tobacco shreds on the white flap. The lens revealed that something else was present as well as the familiar brown shreds.

'There are greenish fragments of what looks like some kind of leaf among the tobacco,' I said. 'Like green tea or a herbal tobacco.'

'Precisely,' he said. 'While Sergeant Bullington made tea for his visitor, they took the opportunity to add to his tobacco jar a pinch of the dried leaves of *Apocynaceae nerium*. If the police at Swindon ever get around to examining West's twist of tobacco, they will find that he died in the same fashion.'

'What on earth is *Apocynaceae nerium*?' I asked.

'It is the oleander, a decorative shrub of the

dogbane family of the Gentianes order—a fiercely poisonous plant, every part of which, roots, stems, leaves, flowers, juice and seeds, is likely to be fatal to anyone who swallows them. It is much used in India as a means of suicide or murder.'

'It is an Indian plant, then?' I said.

'It is,' he agreed, 'but it is widespread among horticulturists in this country and in the United States and Europe. So it would not be difficult for a poisoner to acquire it.'

'It would not be difficult for George Devaux to acquire it,' I said.

'No, indeed,' said Holmes, 'and another place where it may be found is, I suggest, in that jar of Arcadia mixture.'

He bent and picked up the fallen tobacco jar and unscrewed its lid.

'But I imagined that you had brought that from London,' I said. 'You knew that I had not been able to obtain it at the village shop.'

He shook his head. 'Then your imagining was illogical, Watson. You heard me arrive from the station as you were noisily bathing in here. You know that I went straight to my own room. Therefore the jar was placed in here before your bath and before I returned from London. I suggest that you have a word with the landlord as to whence it came, because my lens reveals that I was correct. This too contains oleander fragments.'

I stared at him, appalled by the narrowness

with which I had escaped death.

'You should really be more careful, Watson, with a poisoner at large.'

22

THE CRYING OF THE NECK

There was no discovering the means by which the jar of tobacco had been delivered. Like the parcel at the Swindon workhouse, it had appeared on the bar of the John Barleycorn accompanied by a note stating that it was for 'Dr Wilson.' The landlord, who knew of my efforts to obtain Arcadia mixture, had assumed that the village shop had acquired some and sent it along. Naturally he felt no hesitation in sending his boy to place it in our dressing-room. We had learned nothing new, save that our killer was prepared to attack us and had a knowledge of vegetable poisons.

The harvest proceeded apace. In our first days in Weston Stacey, Holmes and I had given credibility to our assumed characters by going about the village during the day, calling on the older folk and noting their quaint stories, sayings and songs, but there was now no point. All in the village who could walk, from toddling children to old gaffers on two sticks, made their way each day to the harvest fields, if only to watch as the corn was brought in, and Holmes and I took to the same pursuit.

As day after sunny day passed I admit that I was well content to sit in the shade at a corner of a field and watch the age old process. Mr Grainger, the farmer at Toadneck Farm, brought in no machines, so that, when the reapers arrived on his land, we could see the corn cut as it must have been cut for hundreds of years.

When the dew was off the corn in the morning, a row of reapers would form along one side of a field, most of the men bearing big, glinting scythes. At each end of the line were younger men, armed with sickles and a stick—'riphook and fagging stick' as they called them. These were to stoop and cut the shorter, irregular corn that lay along the edges of the planting, where seed had fallen on the 'headland' where the plough turned.

As the line moved into the field, felling the corn in rhythmic sweeps of the blade, women and children—often the wives and children of the reaper—walked behind. The older children lifted the cut stalks into bundles, passing them to their mother, who would form them into sheaves. The younger children ran to and from the nearest brook, bringing strands of straw that had been set to soak there, which their mother could use to bind the sheaves. Older boys and girls helped their mothers stack the sheaves at intervals across the field or followed with a rake, after the carts had collected the sheaves, to pick up any last strands of corn that had been left lying.

Mr Platt, the Harvest Lord, sat under a hedge or walked across behind the line, his eyes everywhere, chivvying where one group of workers had fallen behind the others. To the right of the scythesmen worked the 'Harvest Lady,' Platt's prime reaper. If a reaper required a halt to take out his sharpening stone and put a new edge on his blade, he must call out to Wells, the Harvest Lady, who would halt the line. A few strokes of the stone, two quick shouts and the line would move off again, as orderly as well-drilled soldiers.

All of the village, as I have said, was there each day. The Reverend Trentham went among the old folk sitting in the shade, while his niece, attired in a bright lemon-yellow dress, flitted about among the children like a great butterfly, stopping childish squabbles or picking up an infant who had stumbled and scraped an arm or leg on the new-cut stubble. If she could not staunch their bleeding or their tears, she would often bring them to me for a little medical attention and I was pleased to enjoy her visits to our corner.

Despite the seriousness of our enquiry, I was still deeply appreciative of these days of opportunity to recall my country boyhood and watch the harvest brought in as it had been since time immemorial. Holmes, I suspected, would be deeply bored by the whole process, but to my astonishment, after an initial period of fretfulness, he seemed to enjoy himself every bit as much as I did. He would sprawl in the grass for hours, lens in hand, deeply engrossed in the structure of a weed taken from the hedgerow, or fascinated by the action of some tiny insect among the grass. Often I had to shake his shoulder to make him aware of the 'four o'clock' when refreshments were brought to the field and the work paused.

The weather remained unremittingly fair and hot and the reaping proceeded with little incident other than an occasional cut finger on a scythe or sickle or a touch too much of the burning sun, until what everybody believed would be the last day of reaping. Though that morning dawned as bright as any, a fitful breeze began to come and go during the morning and grey clouds massed on the western horizon. More than once I saw a reaper, pausing to wipe his brow, take a glance at the sky before resuming his work.

As the day advanced the gathering clouds drew further across the sky and their colour deepened to an ominous purple-grey. Still, no drop of rain fell and at last the final field was cut, the wheat bundled into sheaves and stacked in tidy rows. Only a plaited twist of wheat stood at one end of the field. Now a cry went across the field.

'The goose's neck!' somebody called, and every voice, children and adults took it up.

The reapers and their women followers were all gathered a few feet from the plaited clump of wheat. Now everybody else, including the oldest gaffer on sticks, made their way over the stubble to join the group in front of the 'neck.' The Reverend Trentham and his niece were present, and I saw him leading the group in a prayer.

Holmes levered himself up from the grass. 'Come, Watson,' he said. 'I fear that from this moment the danger increases.'

'But to whom?' I said.

'I wish that I knew,' he said, 'but I do not. All we can do to prevent another tragedy is to watch and be alert to anything in the least suspicious.'

We joined the group and watched as each reaper took a sickle and flung it at the lone clump, every failed attempt being met with jeers and cat-calls from the bystanders.

At last one young man caught the neck squarely in the curve of his thrown sickle and felled it. Instantly he sprang to it, snatched it up and held it high. Now the crowd cried, 'The neck! The neck! Us has'n! Us has'n!' and spread apart to form two long lines.

The clouds had now almost entirely obscured the sun, but a few beams still shone down, lighting the strange performance in the cornfield like a searchlight. Still clutching the neck, the man who had brought it down walked to the far end of the two rows of his fellows and charged between them.

As he ran, the bystanders flailed at him with bunches of straw held in their hands and a strange, ululating cry, wordless and meaningless, rose from their throats. I admit that the sound of that strange cry, ringing across the fields under the threatening clouds, made me shiver, and I could not help reflecting that in the past, the man running between the reapers might really have been running for his life.

In seconds it was over and their quarry was away, racing for the open field gate while only a few of the younger lads ran after him.

'Come on now!' shouted Grainger the farmer. 'You've had your fun, now get them carts away before the weather breaks!'

The group broke up and soon the field was a scene of frantic industry again, as every able-bodied man, woman or child sought to get the last two carts loaded and back to the yard before the threatened rain. When this was done, the carters led their horses out of the field accompanied by a ragged cheer. Each cart carried a score of children, scrambling among the load or hanging from its tailboard.

As the carts rumbled into the lane, everyone in the field began to drift towards the gate.

'Be watchful!' warned Holmes. 'The children with the carts are safe. They will ride to the farmyard for the Feast, but keep your eyes out for any child who leaves alone.'

We watched like hawks as every child left

the field, then we walked along behind them. No child had left on its own and none parted from the group who were making their way to Toadneck Farm.

The afternoon grew darker and more gloomy as we walked and, by the time we reached the farm, there were lanterns lit and hanging in one of the barns. The building itself had been swept and decorated with paper chains and twists of corn-straw. Three long tables had been set out in a U shape, the open end towards the door. Each was heaped with plates of food, and jugs of cider, ale and lemonade were spaced along them between the plates.

Adults and children were taking their places along the side tables, while at the end table sat Henry Devaux, Farmer Grainger and his wife, the Reverend Trentham and his niece, and a number of other local dignitaries. The last carts of corn had been stacked with lightning speed and the labourers poured in from the yard and joined the throng around the tables.

Holmes and I were looking for convenient seats which would permit us to keep an unobtrusive eye on people's movements when I spied a familiar but surprising face.

'Look!' I exclaimed to Holmes. 'There's Hayter and his son over there.'

'The infernal idiot!' said Holmes, and pushed his way through the crowd until he was by the man and boy.

'I understood,' he said to Hayter, 'that you were not returning until the harvest was over in Weston Stacey.'

'Nor I wasn't,' Hayter replied, 'but 'tis over, isn't it? It's all in now and Billy did so want to be with his friends for the Feast, so we come up this morning to be here.'

'Mr Hayter,' said Holmes, 'your son is still in very grave danger. I urge you never to let him out of your sight for a moment. Nor should you leave here when the Feast is over except in my company.'

'Why?' asked the labourer. 'What is it you reckon is going to happen to our Billy?'

'If he is not carefully watched,' said Holmes, 'he is very likely to be killed the way that little Bea Collins was killed a year ago.'

That seemed to sober the man. 'Well then,' he said, 'I'll look out for him.'

'And do not leave without letting me know,' repeated Holmes. We seated ourselves at table, where we could keep our eyes on the Hayters.

'There is,' said my friend, 'one outstanding advantage in Hayter's stupidity.'

'What is that?' I asked. 'Surely he has risked his boy's life unnecessarily?'

'So he has,' replied Holmes, 'but by so doing he has made virtually certain who is intended to be the next victim and has thereby made our task a great deal easier.'

Mr Grainger rose in his place and banged the table for silence, then introduced the

216

Reverend Trentham, who blessed the harvest at length and invited all present to join in the singing of 'We Plough the Fields and Scatter the Good Seed on the Land.' Once the old hymn was sung, lustily enough to shake the dust from the rafters above us, Henry Devaux said a few words and then the Feast was under way.

The days of fresh air and sunshine had given me almost as brisk an appetite as those who had laboured in the sun, and I ate and drank with the best of them, but I did not forget to keep an eye on young Hayter, who sat a little way along on the other side of our table, laughing with a tall, red-haired boy.

The pies and pastries, sandwiches and cakes, had all vanished, the tables been cleared and the jugs of ale and cider and lemonade replenished. Now pipes and cigarettes were got out and the company began to sing choruses as one after another of the labourers sang a song. Laughter, chatter and song flowed up to the rafters along with the smoke of pipes and cigarettes.

'I have barns, I have bowers,
I have birds, I have flowers,
And the lark is my morning alarmer,
So me jolly boys, now,
Here's God speed the plough,
Long life and success to the farmer.'

The whole company was roaring out the old

chorus when a burst of white light lit the whole courtyard outside, glowing into the barn and washing the sun-burned faces of the revellers white. An instant later a clap of thunder rang right overhead and a great gust of wind battered at the doors, rattling them on their hinges. Straw and chaff from the yard blew into the barn. Outside the sky was nearly as dark as night, only a vivid yellow streak low on the horizon showing that the sun still shone. Hardly had we recovered from the wind's buffeting when a curtain of rain lashed across the yard outside.

Farmer Grainger was on his feet in an instant. 'Come on, lads!' he called. 'Outside and look to the stacks! Make sure the sheeting holds!'

The company broke up in confusion. Men and lads were spilling out of the door, plunging through the rain towards the stackyard. Some were pulling on oilskins that had appeared from somewhere, others merely flung a sack across their head and shoulders while some went bare-headed into the downpour.

Striving to keep watch over Billy Hayter, I saw him and his red-headed friend dragging on oilskins and I watched them run to a stack. His father I saw, slumped half senseless at the table. From the door of the barn I was able to keep a little out of the rain's way and mark the boy's movements around the stacks, Billy's friend's hair serving as a useful indicator. Holmes stood close behind me, peering over my head.

'Surely,' I said to him, 'our killer will not strike in this?'

'It might have been made for murder,' he said. 'Darkness, pouring rain, a confused crowd of men and boys—keep close watch, Watson. I fear we are very near to time.'

The rain kept up but the confusion was sorting itself out. Soon the men and boys were working steadily at the stacks, checking the tarpaulins, replacing those that had been disturbed by the wind, retying loosened knots and bringing extra canvases to cover the western sides of the stacks, where the rain was beating.

Soon it was all done and the workers began to drift back into the barn. I relaxed, seeing the red-haired boy and a group of others heading towards us. Beside me, on the barn door, a soaked fragment of Miss Thorne's Festivities poster flapped in the breeze.

'It is a pity,' I remarked to Holmes, 'that we shall not be here to see Miss Thorne's Curiosities. With her outspokenness, they might be very interesting.'

'Miss Thorne's Curiosities?' Holmes repeated. 'What are you talking about, Watson?'

He was silent for a moment, then I felt him move and, turning, saw that he was staring wildly about the great barn.

'Where is Billy Hayter?' he demanded.

'Why,' I said, 'he's over there with his friend,' and I walked across to where I could see the red-headed youth unbuttoning his oilskin.

'Where's Billy?' I asked the boy.

'He's not here, sir,' he said. 'He went when he got the message—straightaway.'

23

THE GODDESS OF DEATH

'The message! What message?' demanded Holmes.

'Why, sir, he said as his Mum was sick and he must go. He left me holding the rope, he went so quick.'

'Where is his mother sick?' Holmes asked.

'He said as he was going back to Buckstone, sir.'

'Buckstone!' snapped Holmes. 'Watson, we have been defeated. The boy has been taken away from before our very eyes. We must have a fast trap.'

We looked around us, seeking anyone who might have transport. Holmes strode down the barn to where Henry Devaux sat chatting to the vicar.

'Mr Devaux,' he said, 'another child has

been taken. Have you a carriage or trap outside? We may be able to save him yet.'

'Another!' exclaimed Devaux. 'Why, yes, Mr Holmes. My trap is at the front of the farm.' He rose quickly. 'I'll come with you,' he said. 'Where's my groom?'

He cast a glance around the barn, spotted his groom at a table and summoned him with a bellow of, 'Harris! The trap!'

The groom leapt to his feet and all three of us plunged after him through the blinding rain along a path through the farm gardens to the road. Helter-skelter we tumbled into the trap as the groom whipped up his horse.

'Where to, sir?' he asked his master.

'Buckstone,' replied Holmes, 'as fast as you can!'

We started out at a rattling pace. The hedgerows were high with late summer growth and branches and leaves sprang at us as we passed, the road surface was awash from the driving rain so that our equipage lurched occasionally over hollows and ruts and I could not help but fear that we would overturn or break a wheel. Nevertheless our driver kept up a remarkable speed and held to the road until we rounded a bend that brought the Mayfield into our view.

Peering through the rain we could see that a trap stood unattended in the lane beside the stile. Two figures wrapped in oilskins were climbing over the stile. The shorter was clearly the Hayter boy, but the taller, its head and shoulders wrapped with a sack, was unrecognisable to me at a distance and in the blinding rain.

'By the stile!' Holmes commanded the groom. 'Pull in by the stile!'

We sprang from the trap with as little ceremony as we had boarded it and clambered over the stile. It was impossible to run in the Mayfield. The little footpath had become a muddy brook and the stubble alongside was a treacherous surface of wet straw stubs. We floundered up the slight incline, peering anxiously ahead for our quarry. The rain fell so heavily and the gloom was so intense that, although we were only seconds behind them, it was impossible to be sure that they were still on the path ahead of us.

Then a blinding flash of lightning lit the landscape and we could see that the pair were nearing the brow of the rise, close to the little cairn.

'We must stop them!' shouted Holmes, over the thunder. 'Watson! Your pistol!'

I dragged my Adams from my pocket as the thunder rolled and echoed around us.

'Billy!' cried Holmes, cupping his hands to his mouth. 'Billy Hayter!'

The boy turned, but his companion dragged at his arm and spun him around.

'Get away!' called Holmes. 'Run for your life!'

Again the boy turned and again his companion dragged him round. This time a second lunge broke the taller figure's grasp and for a moment the boy was free, but his captor spun and grabbed him with an arm across Billy's chest.

I had raised my pistol, but the rain was lashing straight into my face and I dared not risk a shot for fear of hitting the boy.

We had been stumbling steadily nearer to the pair and could now see them much more clearly. Billy, it seemed, was still struggling to free himself but was restrained by the arm around his chest. Suddenly the tall figure flung up its other arm and tore the sacking from its head and shoulders. With another movement of the hand it dragged up some kind of hood or mask from inside the bosom of its oilskin coat. In an instant we were faced with the demon figure that had appeared at the Buckstone.

The struggling boy had wriggled lower to escape the hold on him and suddenly he dropped, slithering out of his over-sized oilskin in one move and freeing himself. Desperately he flung himself forward, but slipped on the muddy path and sprawled face forward to the ground.

His erstwhile captor now ripped the oilskin away from its body, to reveal the patterned robe and the pendant skulls. Snatching something from its bosom, it flung up its left arm and gave vent to a blood-chilling cry as it advanced a pace towards the helpless boy.

Nothing, I believed, could save little Billy now but my pistol. Steadying my firing hand with the other arm, I tried to centre on the horrifying figure that towered over its victim. The lashing rain blurred my vision, but I knew that I must try.

Two events occurred simultaneously. I squeezed the trigger to fire a shot that I was almost certain would not find its mark and, in the same instant, a dazzling, ragged streak of lightning ran down the sky out of the boiling blackness above. As I tried to centre a second shot the lightning found its mark, striking the shining object in the monstrous figure's outstretched hand. There was a huge flare of light at the contact and a hideous shriek from the victim, almost instantaneously muffled by a loud bang.

There was no need of a second shot. The robed and masked figure fell and lay still as we scrambled towards it.

We reached Billy first. He still lay face down on the muddy footpath, his hands tightly clasped over his ears, shaking with fright and sodden through.

' "And the Lord sent thunder and hail and the fire ran along upon the ground",' quoted a voice behind me. It was Harris, Devaux's groom, who had come up behind us.

'Thank you, Harris,' snapped Devaux. 'We

can do without the hail.'

I was able to confirm in a very rapid check that he had come to no physical harm and asked Devaux's groom to take the boy to the trap and wrap him in a rug. Devaux contributed his pocket brandy flask to the lad's welfare and we moved to examine Billy's captor.

That the villain was dead was plain. The lightning had struck the object in the left hand, a silver ornamented weapon of some kind, and had found its way to earth through the right foot, the soaking shoe of which had been blasted from the seared foot. Much of its force would have passed through the region of the heart and killed instantly.

Holmes lifted the grotesque mask and wig from the head, revealing the pale face of Cecily Thorne, fixed in a hideous grimace but otherwise unmarked.

I was astounded. 'Miss Thorne!' I exclaimed. But you never suggested, Holmes . . .'

He had turned the dead woman's head gently between his hands.

'I should have known,' he interrupted me. 'I should have known. Look, she wore no earrings.'

The comment made no sense at all to me. I confirmed my impression that she was dead and stood silently by as Holmes stooped over the body, like some great bird of prey under that dramatic sky. He touched, very gingerly, the still hot remains of the object that she had held aloft, then reached into her patterned robe at the waist, drawing out a length of fine black material with a knotted corner. He drew out his pocket-knife and cut the skulls free, wrapping them with the mask and her weapon in the cloth, then straightened himself and stood for a moment as the rain poured down his pale face.

'There is nothing more to be done here,' he said at last. 'It is ended.'

We covered her with the cast-off oilskins and, as the rain began to slacken and the thunder grew faster and more distant, we rode slowly back to Weston Stacey under the last fitful light of that extraordinary day.

24

INDIAN CURIOSITIES

Holmes' long fingers smoothed the telegram form upon the table.

'If this,' he said, 'had arrived a little earlier, it would have made my task a great deal easier, saved the Hayter boy a terrifying experience and probably saved the life of Cecily Thorne.'

'I still find it hard to believe that what we have witnessed in Weston Stacey was the work of Miss Thorne,' I said.

We were seated in the parlour of the John Barleycorn and had just finished breakfast when our landlord had brought the telegram and PC Russell to us.

Holmes smiled thinly at me. 'Good old Watson!' he said. 'Ever the romantic! Your melodramatic tastes evidently extend beyond your own works. I'll wager you would have had poor George Devaux as a villain in a trice, rather than believe that a personable young woman, devoted to good works and the daughter of missionaries, should be an insane killer. If reality were as simple as melodrama, there would be hardly any need for detectives.'

'I had thought that Devaux was a likely suspect,' I said.

Holmes nodded. 'A strange and wealthy invalid, with a taste for exotic and unpleasant plants—I see your thinking, but you ignored what your medically trained eyes must have told you.'

'What was that?' I asked.

'That his limp was not feigned and that his sickly complexion was not the product of dye or make-up. Could a man as sick as Devaux have been the organiser and executioner for our killers?'

'I also considered Platt,' I said.

'There, Watson, you are displaying a prejudice against our Harvest Lord because of his curious calling, which, you will admit, he pursues with as much humanity as commerce

227

permits. No, Platt gave me a valuable piece of information. You recall that it was he who referred us to the Yetcham case? He also dropped a hint which I was slow to take up. He warned me of "deceivers".'

'I remember,' I said. 'What did he mean?'

'He meant that he suspected some form of Thuggee. "Deceivers" is the meaning of Thugs.'

'I do not understand this about Thuggee,' said PC Russell.

'You shall do,' promised Holmes, 'but let me take things in order. When you first consulted me I was able, without further data, to tell you that the killing of Beatrice Collins was unusual in that it was not prompted by any of the three principal motives for murder— lust, greed or revenge. What is more, the use of two completely distinct weapons, one of them very unusual, suggested to me an element of ritual in the affair.'

He paused, took out his briar pipe and filled it. When it was well alight he continued.

'When I visited the Mayfield, I found a fragment of sugar paper near the scene of little Bea's death. It need not have been significant, but it was an odd item to discover in the middle of a field.'

'What did it mean, Mr Holmes?' asked Russell.

'Very little, at that time,' said my friend. 'It was after Platt's story of the Berkshire crime, when we went to Yetcham, that my suspicions began to crystallise. There we found an almost identical killing, save only that the Berkshire victim was a boy. The death had occurred on the last day of a harvest, at a place formerly of ritual significance to the villagers. Once again the victim had been first stunned with a highly individual weapon, then strangled, and once again there was sugar found at the scene.'

He paused and looked at us as though expecting questions. We had none, so he went on.

'Sugar once might have been an accident, but sugar twice was not. Now, I have read widely in the literature of crime, but I had never heard of more than one use of sugar by killers and that was among the Thugs who took what they called "consecrated sugar" before any major venture—you saw them take it in ritual fashion at the Buckstone, Watson, before they passed sentence on the hapless West.'

The recollection of that unholy communion chilled me.

'In addition,' continued Holmes, 'at Yetcham there was a blank metal disc found close to the dead boy. Now, it may have had no greater significance than the broken toy also found on the path, but it occurred to me that it might well be the weight used instead of a coin in the corner of the rumal—the strangling cloth of a Thug.'

'But have there ever been Thug murders in

England before?' I asked.

Holmes shook his head. 'Not so far as I can determine,' he said, 'and at first I was very loath to accept what the evidence suggested. What forced me to recognise the pattern of the data was the use of two weapons. Apart from the rumal with which they strangled, the Thugs also carried the khussee—a small ritual pickaxe, an implement which would inflict the distinctive wounds found on both of the victims.'

'I still don't understand about the Thugs, Mr Holmes,' complained Constable Russell.

Holmes smiled. 'I do not imagine that the history of Thuggee is part of a rural policeman's training,' he said, and went on to outline the story of the cult much as Devaux had given it to us.

'But you say they were stamped out three generations ago, Mr Holmes?'

Holmes shook his head. 'Thuggee was practised from end to end of India, even by pirate boat crews at sea. Sleeman's efforts resulted in the arrest, conversion, transportation or hanging of some three thousand. I recall that some of them even wove a carpet for Queen Victoria to prove their conversion to honest industry. Nevertheless, there must have been thousands of adherents who were never detected and in some of them the old savage faith would smoulder on.'

'But how did it come to Weston Stacey?' asked the young officer.

'That depended solely on Weston Stacey being the home of the Devauxs,' said Holmes. 'We know that Sergeant Bullington, Cecily Thorne and her parents, Platt the gangmaster and the Devauxs were all in Tokot at the same time. Devaux has told us that he offered the living of Weston Stacey to Cecily's uncle and that he encouraged both Bullington and Platt to come to this area.'

'There seems to be nothing untoward in that,' said Russell. 'It seems to have been kindly meant.'

'I'm sure it was,' agreed Holmes, 'but its effect was to bring to Weston Stacey the old contagion of Thuggee from India, and here it grafted itself on to the native stock, the local pagan survivals and superstitions.'

'But how?' I asked. 'Surely the two things are distinct?'

'Mischance played a great part in events,' said Holmes. 'We know that in India Sergeant Bullington became such a drunkard that his rank was threatened, until he was helped by Miss Thorne's father. We know that he repaid their kindness when an epidemic of fever struck Tokot, by bringing to Cecily's aid his Indian mistress, a woman apparently deeply skilled in native healing arts, who saved the girl's life.'

I recalled the framed photograph in Bullington's home. 'Of course!' I said. 'There was a picture of her in his sitting-room.'

'You are most probably right,' agreed Holmes, 'and that, in itself, is unusual. All over the Empire soldiers, sailors and administrators seek the consolations of native women, but when their tour of duty is over they return home to marry, or to their existing wives, and their foreign indiscretions are a sealed book thereafter. Sergeant Bullington not only never married when he returned to England, but gave that photograph of an Indian woman pride of place in his home. I agree with you, Watson, that the photograph is almost certainly of his native lover.'

'Are you suggesting,' I asked, 'that Cecily Thorne became involved with Thuggee through Sergeant Bullington's woman?'

'How more easily?' asked Holmes. 'A young girl, suddenly deprived of her parents in a foreign land, brought to death's door by disease and restored to life by the skills of that woman—would she not see her saviour as almost a guardian angel? And would not a native woman who had guarded the forbidden secrets of Thuggee take an especial delight in casting her influence over a child of Christian missionaries?'

'Yes,' I said, 'that makes a deal of sense.'

'There is a further point. Would you not agree with me, Doctor, that survivors of violent fevers sometimes prove to have suffered permanent damage to the brain?'

I nodded. 'Yes,' I said. 'We do not know

232

what was the disease that carried off her parents and from which she recovered, but there are a number of tropical infections that can leave lasting damage to the brain.'

'Thank you,' he said. 'It is my experience that among those fortunately rare people who kill more than once, there are some who seem to have suffered damage to the brain through disease or accident and others who are congenitally damaged. Consider, then, that when Cecily Thorne returned from India she may have been both subverted in her faith by her Indian mentor and damaged in her mind by the disease, and she came here, to Weston Stacey, a village where strange and ancient rituals are played out which echo the blood sacrifices once demanded each harvest-time.'

'Mr Holmes,' said Constable Russell, doggedly, 'all this fits together very nicely and makes a great deal of sense where there wasn't none before, but I can't understand why you say that she tied Thuggism or Thuggee as you call it together with the old harvest practices. They aren't the same thing, are they?'

'That's right,' I said. 'The Thugs were robbers, who killed to steal. If there was killing in the old days to guarantee a good harvest next year, that was a sacrifice.'

Holmes smiled. 'You are both right,' he said, 'and I balked at the same problem, but a large part of the answer lies in the identity of Kali, the Thugs' goddess of death.'

'She was Durga, the wife of Shiva,' I said. 'She was the embodiment of the principle of creation and destruction in Hindu belief, surely.'

'Well done, Watson. Quite right,' he said. 'She was the "Dark Mother" of the Thugs, who exalted her negative, destructive side, in the same way that black magicians in Europe worship the dark aspects of the Mother Goddess. When Cecily Thorne returned to England she looked for, and found, an English version of the worship of the Mother—in the half-forgotten, distorted, and now harmless rituals of the farm labourers. From that mixture she wove her dreadful fantasy and made it an even more dreadful reality. Here also she found Sergeant Bullington, a man with official authority over the villagers and probably a willing lieutenant in preserving the faith that his lost lover held.'

'Was it she, then, who poisoned the sergeant?' I asked.

'Definitely,' said Holmes. 'After the fracas in Buckstone Wood and the escape of West, he will have consulted her. She feared exposure, not least from the sergeant or one of his group. A pinch of oleander in his tobacco jar solved her problem, reinforced discipline among her followers and left her to deal with West by the same means.'

'But how did she know that West was in Swindon?' I asked. 'PC Russell told me almost as soon as he knew.'

'I can answer that,' said the constable. 'I heard by telegraph from Swindon. Miss Thorne was kind enough to deliver the telegram from the post office. Just doing her friend Miss Walters at the post office a favour, she said.'

I was thinking of the deaths of West and the sergeant, let alone the attempt on my own life.

'She was a daring woman,' I commented.

'A cool, intelligent, woman,' said Holmes, 'who might have become whatever she wished but for her madness. I cannot but admire her behaviour at the Feast.'

'Admire!' I exclaimed.

'Admire,' he repeated. 'Her time for sacrifice had come and she was determined that Billy Hayter would be her victim, so as to stop him drawing further attention to the Buckstone, but she knew that we were watching the boy. She must have been burning with frustration, but the sudden storm gave her the opportunity she sought. Already clad in her ritual robe and with her mask and weapons hidden about her, it was the work of a moment to slip into a large oilskin, remove her dress in that dark yard, and then mingle with all the other unrecognisable figures in oilskins and sacking. Why should Billy fear the vicar's niece with a message about his mother?'

He knocked out his pipe and pocketed it. 'There was a further element,' he said. 'Do you recall, Watson, that Henry Devaux spoke of an outbreak of selling and killing children in Tokot?'

'Yes,' I said, 'I do. What was that about?'

'I paid it little attention at the time but while I was in London I called at the offices of the missionary society which employed Cecily's father. My intention was to find if there were retired missionaries in England who had been in Tokot at that time and they provided me with a list. I was also able to speak to one of their longest-serving India hands about child murder in India. She explained to me that there is a superstition among some low-caste Hindus that the death of a child, sacrificed to Kali, will bring good fortune. It tends to surface, it seems, during bad harvests and times of poverty, when people will slaughter their own children to propitiate the goddess or sell them to be slaughtered by others.'

'Then you had the final link between the English beliefs and the Indian,' I said.

'Exactly,' he said, 'but much as I may twit you about your romantic sensibilities, Watson, everything in me fought against identifying Cecily Thorne as the originator of the harvest murders. Thuggee, access to the ossuary at the church, these meant nothing, but the poisoning should have made me alert. It is very much a feminine art. Until the very end I tried to convince myself that it might yet be one of the Devauxs or even Platt. It was your remarks about the poster that focused my thoughts, as you have done so often, my friend.'

'My remarks?' I said. 'I have forgotten what I said.'

'You remarked on the advertisement for Miss Thorne's "Indian Curiosities". It provoked two trains of thought. Firstly I realised that Cecily Thorne, when identifying us by our correct names over her uncle's tea-table, had shown absolutely no curiosity about the reasons for our covert presence in the village—an extraordinary reaction from a woman of any kind, let alone one as forthright and intelligent as she. Secondly I realised that she displayed a physical curiosity—she wore no ear-rings.'

Russell and I looked at each other blankly then at Holmes.

'It is another of my observations,' he said, 'that among persons who kill more than once are a number who have certain distinguishing physical characteristics, among which are the absence of lobes to the ears.'

I recalled how fast my trivial comment had been processed by his remarkable brain and turned into action, and I marvelled again at his singular mental facilities. It seemed I was not the only one.

'Mr Holmes,' said PC Russell, in tones of the greatest awe, 'if I hadn't heard it all from your own mouth, I do not know that I could have believed it.'

Holmes smiled at the young man. 'It is merely a refined capacity for observing small details, allied to the application of logic,' he said.

'However,' I said, 'you have not told us about Yetcham. How came the boy to be killed there?'

He picked up the telegram again. 'I said earlier that this might have saved time and risk. It also explains the connection. In London the missionary society gave me the addresses of retired missionaries from Tokot. Among them was a Miss Victoria Burton, who lived at Reading.'

He laid the telegram form before us. I could see that it said:

MISS THORNE DAUGHTER OF VICAR WESTON STACEY VISITS MISS BURTON RETIRED MISSIONARY AT YETCHAM STOP NO OTHER REGULAR CONNECTION TRACED

It was signed by the inspector at Yetcham.

'So she was visiting Yetcham at the hay harvest?' I said.

'Exactly,' said Holmes. 'Miss Burton has changed her address. Cecily Thorne had successfully accomplished a sacrifice at Weston last August and there she was, present at another harvest. The poison in her blood must have bubbled as she felt that the time was

238

right for another sacrifice. There had to be a victim at Yetcham.'

We all fell silent a while, then PC Russell spoke.

'What can I tell my superiors, Mr Holmes? They will never believe all this!'

'Last night,' said Holmes, 'I told Henry Devaux much of the truth. He is a justice of the Peace, I suggest you accept his guidance. It is singular, is it not, that you consulted me because of your concern that your sergeant appeared to have concealed a murder confession, and now I advise you to take part in the concealment of at least five murders?'

The young policeman shook his head. 'Nevertheless, I think you may well be right, Mr Holmes—so long as there are no more murders.'

'There will be no more murders,' said Holmes. 'Platt's child labourers may go about their business with no more to fear than long hours, bad weather and long, hard roads, but there will be no more murders.'

Holmes and I caught a London train that afternoon. It was not one of the bright, sunlit days to which we had become accustomed, but a muggy, grey day with the sky entirely overcast. From the window of our compartment I saw that the trackside streams, brown and sluggish when we had travelled west, were now full and running freely. The wide water meadows of the Thames valley had recovered their lush green after the long hot spell.

'And it has come just in time for the fruit harvest,' remarked Holmes.

'Holmes!' I complained. 'You are reading my thoughts again!'

He laughed. 'As always, Watson, I was merely following your eyes and your expression, but it is true that the hot spell has broken at exactly the right time.'

'I never knew you to take such an interest in country matters,' I said.

'Perhaps you have converted me, Watson. For all the grimness of our investigation at Weston Stacey, I recognise that you have derived a good deal of pleasure from our country interlude.'

I could not deny it.

'Well then,' he continued, 'since I am contemplating retirement and since I could not reasonably remain in London without practising, I may have to learn to look with kindness on the countryside. This investigation has revealed to me my limitations, Watson. I grow older and, it seems, less responsive to data and more a prey to irrational emotion.'

It was the first time I had ever heard him mention retirement in any serious way.

'But you have years yet!' I protested.

He shook his head. 'I am approaching my half-century, Watson, and half of my life has been spent in promoting the idea of scientific detection and rational analysis. I have, perhaps, gone so far as I may. The younger men at Scotland Yard have begun to adopt some of my methods and science has come to their assistance. Do you recall the day we first met? I believed I had found a reliable reagent for human blood. I turned out to be wrong, but now there is one, thanks to Uhlenhuth's work, as well as a reliable reagent for human semen. Galion and Henry, Herschel and Faulds have systematised fingerprints, which will be of the first importance in criminal investigation in years to come. For once the stick-in-the-muds at the Yard have adopted a worthwhile system and it will give them rich results. No, Watson, I fear the time has come to withdraw from the field and leave it to these new scientific Scotland Yarders.'

'But you have always criticised the Scotland Yarders,' I said.

He shook his head. 'Not all, Watson, not all of them. Toby Gregson and some of that generation will do very well and go far. It is time for me to leave them to it.'

I was dumbfounded. I could not believe that after a quarter of a century of his practice, he was so ready to end it, but so it proved to be. There were other cases after the Weston Stacey affair, but in little more than a year Holmes had been as good as his word and gone into that retirement which he still enjoys. I cannot help believing that his decision was premature and that London in particular, and

England at large, still needs his unofficial talents and his astonishing deductions.

The grotesque events at Weston Stacey never reached the ears of the public and Holmes was right in his assertion that the killings had ended. Without their leader the villagers turned away from the insanity she had brought, most probably deeply frightened by the manner of her death. Her uncle relinquished the living of Weston Stacey and took up missionary work, not in India, but in the slums of a manufacturing city. His obituary appeared in the press some years ago. If it had not, I would not have felt able to pen this account of the killings in 1902. As it is, I still feel it best to leave it unpublished until no blame can be visited on anyone in that charming village.

Editor's Notes

As explained in my introductory Note, I have made such efforts as seemed reasonable to try and establish the authenticity of this manuscript. It is right that I should record here a debt of gratitude to Philip Gardner of Beaconsfield, Bucks, without whose assistance some of the following information would not have reached me.

The first difficulty which bedevils any enquiry into the authenticity of an alleged Watson manuscript is the lack of any absolutely proven example of Watson's handwriting. Colour reproductions of what are said to be a number of documents written by Watson appear in the Peerage Books edition of *A Study in Scarlet* (London, Webb & Bower, 1983). That volume is not the text as Watson published it, but claims to be (and may indeed be) a complete reproduction of the notes, cuttings, journal entries, etc. on which Watson founded his published account. The longer journal entries are in typescript on buff or pink quarto paper but the book includes the following in Watson's hand:

Title page	Black ink and pencil on buff scrapbook page
Diary notes	Black ink on blue lined pages

	from 8" x 5.75" notebook
Personal letter	Black ink on cream headed notepaper
Memorandum	Violet ink on pale lavender unheaded notepaper

These documents seem authentic, but Larry Millett asserts in a note to *Sherlock Holmes and the Red Demon* (Viking, New York, 1996) that the Watson manuscript from which he extracted his text was on foolscap paper bearing the watermark of Eynsford Paper Mills. It was written, he says, with a Koh-I-Noor pencil, made from distinctive Siberian graphite and known to be a favourite of Watson's after it was introduced in 1890. Watson, he claims, would write his first draft in pencil, then send it to be typed. Millett also claims to know of six other Watson manuscripts in the same format.

Now it is highly unlikely that both Millett and Simon Goodenough (who made the *Study in Scarlet* papers available to Peerage Books) are right—the differences are too many and too great. Admittedly, the Koh-I-Noor pencil was not available when Watson wrote A *Study in Scarlet,* but that volume shows a preference for black ink, tinted notepapers and quarto typing paper whereas Millett would have us believe in pencil on foolscap paper. It would be helpful if I could assert that the manuscripts in my possession match either Goodenough's or Millett's but insofar as I have examined them, they consist of text in blue-black ink on cream, unlined foolscap leaving me unable to assert that they are absolutely definitely the work of John H. Watson, though the handwriting compares well with the Goodenough examples.

Faced with that difficulty, I have sought to confirm by any other means that the present manuscript is authentic. The results which I have achieved are noted below, though it may well be that a reader with more time or greater specialised knowledge of certain aspects of the story may be able to achieve a more positive result. Certainly I am as satisfied as I can be that the story of the Harvest of Death is a previously unknown work by Dr Watson, recording a hitherto unknown investigation by Sherlock Holmes. Readers will, in the end, have to reach their own conclusions.

CHAPTER ONE

The comment about pencils and young ladies from boarding schools may be found in 'The Copper Beeches'.

Watson is referring, of course, to the summer of 1902 when he speaks of the second summer of the century. The twentieth century of the Christian Era began in 1901 and will end in 2000. Despite a popular opinion to the contrary, the Third Millennium will begin in 2001, not 2000.

CHAPTER TWO

May Day was, of course, the original date on which the coming of summer was celebrated, but the Church frowned on this pagan festival and managed to move many of its manifestations forward to Whitsun. So the local Friendly Society at Highclere, Hants, used to organise a procession of white-clad girls to church at Whitsun, followed by a picnic on the Earl of Carnarvon's estate at the imitation Roman temple folly above the lake called Dunsmere or Temple Mere. A postcard from Wolverhampton in 1903 portrays a Whitsun procession of white-clad schoolgirls showing that the custom survived in the heart of the industrial region into this century. Aficionados of unsolved murders will recall Mary Ashton of Sutton Coldfield who was murdered after a Whitsun dance in 1818 (see *Midland Murders and Mysteries*, Barrie Roberts, Quercus, 1997).

Where the incumbent did not object on grounds of temperance or general morality, the village festivals known as 'Ales' were often directly promoted and sponsored by the Church which would purchase the beer in bulk and take the profits into its funds. If they were not marking any special occasion these were known as 'Church Ales.' In the end the temperance lobby won.

CHAPTER THREE

The 'crying of the neck' and other customs surrounding the last sheaf of a harvest are described in Sir James Frazer's *The Golden Bough* (Macmillan, 1922). Sir James appears to have believed that the customs were extinct by the time he wrote, but a film in the possession of the Royal Cornish Institute—'Spirit of Cornwall'—shows the neck being cried in Cornwall in the mid-1920s. Oddly, that film was made at a place called Towednack Farm, a name apparently deriving from 'the old neck' and eerily similar to the name of the farm in Watson's manuscript.

CHAPTER SIX

Holmes refers to the Flying Dutchman and the American Bar, both of which were well-known sailors' pubs in Liverpool in his day. According to Stan Hugill's *Sailortown* (Routledge & Kegan Paul Ltd, London, 1968), they were still standing when he wrote and may well be so today.

The ballad of 'John Barleycorn' was one of the most widespread of British rural songs. Versions have been collected from all over these islands and though they may differ as to seriousness, all versions revolve around the personification of the spirit of the grain in

John Barleycorn. The particular version noted by Watson is very like one which appears in Alfred Williams' *Folk-Songs of the Upper Thames* (Duckworth & Co, London, 1923) and which Williams recorded from an Edward Warren at South Marston, Wiltshire. It helps to convince me that the scene of Watson's narrative is somewhere in northern Wiltshire.

CHAPTER SEVEN

Fanny Adams, an eight-year-old girl, was abducted, murdered and chopped into twenty pieces on 24th August 1867 near Alton, Hants. Her killer was an insane solicitor's clerk called Frederick Baker who was hanged at Winchester on the following Christmas Eve before a crowd of 5,000 spectators. The horrible circumstances of the murder made it a very widely known crime and a ballad was composed which still lives in the mouths of folksingers. The crime took place when the Royal Navy was introducing canned meat to the diet of sailors. Dubious as to the contents of the cans, the matelots generated the joking explanation that the contents were 'Sweet Fanny Adams.' This usage gave rise, in time, to the use of the expression to mean 'absolutely nothing' and as a synonym for a much coarser phrase. As in the present narrative, local people raised a small cairn to mark the spot where Fanny Adams was found. In an article in *Folk Review*

248

in April 1977, C. W. Hawkins revealed that he and Clarence H. Grace had located the cairn in the hedgerow of Horaces Field near to the old hop-gardens in the late 1960s but that it had been obliterated by the Amery Hill School playing field. We know that Watson (born in 1852) spent a part of his youth in Hampshire and there is no reason why he should not have seen Fanny Adams' cairn.

CHAPTER EIGHT

Natives of Portland, Dorset, long connected to the mainland by the famous Chesil Beach, nevertheless refer to themselves as 'islanders.' They also have a superstitious fear of rabbits, refusing even to name them and adopting expressions like 'little furry creatures with long ears' if they need to mention them. Tradition says that the belief that rabbits are bad luck stems from the stoneworkers of Portland's quarries. Rabbits, it seems, would penetrate the stone and weaken it, causing collapses of the quarry face and the death of stone-cutters.

Mumming plays are traditionally presented at Christmas, New Year, Old Christmas Day, or Easter. Two champions fight and one is slain, but revived by a doctor. In most versions of the play St George is one of the protagonists. The other is often the Turkish Knight (sometimes corrupted to 'Turkey Snipe') Prince Saladin or, occasionally, a dragon. An essay on the plays, texts of two and a complete miniature theatre with figures to perform *St George and the Dragon* can be found in *St George and the Dragon* by Peter C. Jackson and Ronald Smedley (Pollock's Toy Theatres Ltd, London, 1972) which I believe is still available from Pollock's shops at Scala Street and Covent Garden.

The vicar's hints at indecent ceremonies connected with planting crops caused me much reading which revealed nothing of the kind recorded in Britain. However, in Richard Chase's *American Folk Tales and Songs* (Signet Key Books, USA, 1956) I found a reference to an article by Vance Randolph in the *Journal of Arkansas Folklore*, Volume 66, Number 262, October-December 1953, called 'Nakedness in Ozark Folk Belief.' Randolph cites a belief that 'certain crops grew better if the persons who sowed the seed were naked . . . Four grown girls and one boy did the planting. They all stripped off naked. The boy started in the middle of the patch with four big girls a-prancing around him. The boy throwed all the seed and the girls kept a-hollerin' "Pxxxer deep! Pxxxer deer!" . . . There ain't no sense to it but them folks always raised the best turnips on the creek . . . Soon as he got their bread planted, [he] would take his wife out to the patch at midnight—take off every stitch of clothes and run round the crop three times. And then he would throw her right down in the dirt and have at it . . . Wash off in the creek and go on back home.' The procedure was said to protect corn from frost, drought, birds and insects. Chase draws comparisons with practices in India and in ancient history. As colonial America drew its traditions from Britain, it may be that this practice, or something like it, was what the Reverend Trentham had in mind.

It is an astonishing proof of the grip which superstition and tradition hold on the public mind that such practices could survive among the fundamentalist Christian communities of America in the mid-1950s. I should be fascinated to know whether they continue to this day (in America or in Britain).

CHAPTER NINE

The harvest gangs were a constant feature of life in rural England in the last century and the early years of this one. A version of the system still survives in some fruit-growing areas, where gang labour is supplied by a contractor. For information on Victorian and Edwardian harvest gangs, I refer you to *Labouring Life in the Victorian Countryside* by Pamela Horn (Gill & MacMillan, Dublin, 1976; Fraser Stewart, Oxon, 1995) and to an article by my late friend David H. Morgan, 'The Place of Harvesters in Nineteenth Century Village Life,' which appears in *Village Life and Labour,* edited by Raphael

Samuel (Routledge & Kegan Paul, 1975).

While you may look in vain for Weston Stacey on any map, you will find Uphusband on an old enough map. It is one of two villages in western Hampshire, formerly known as Uphusband and Downhusband, which took their names from the Hurstbourne ('Harvest stream') river. They are named on modern maps as Hurstbourne and Hurstbourne Tarrant.

CHAPTERS ELEVEN and TWELVE

That a belief in a personal Devil survived in the English countryside well into this century is a matter which I can certify. One Christmas Eve in the late 1950s the wife of a neighbour in the north Hampshire valley where I grew up was terrified out of her wits on meeting what she believed to be Satan as she went out into the dark backyard to fetch coal. Her husband was less surprised and announced that, as a young man working as a hedger-and-ditcher, he had often seen the Devil and opined that 'He won't do you no harm as long as you keeps your eye on him and never turns your back on him.'

Erasmus Darwin's theory on crop circles was set out in a letter to *a* friend *in* 1779. It seems to be insufficiently known, particularly among those who claim to know about crop circles. It is a shame that Holmes was not alive in the 1960s to hear the 'scientific' explanations that greeted the appearance of circles in the reedy lagoons of Queensland, Australia—what would he have made of crocodiles fornicating in mathematical circles or a giant rotating bird, both of which were put forward by 'scientists'?

CHAPTER FOURTEEN

The comment on Colonel Harden is a reference to the case which I have edited as *Sherlock Holmes and the Devil's Grail* (Constable, 1996) and which details the 'singular persecution of Jon Wesley Harden, the American tobacco millionaire.' Both from the manuscript itself and by cross-reference to 'The Solitary Cyclist', it is clear that the Devil's Grail affair occurred in the early summer of 1895. It might be thought that there is a dating error in the present narrative, inasmuch as Professor Moriarty died at the Reichenbach Falls in the spring of 1891, but in the Devil's Grail case Holmes and Watson found themselves pitted against a section of Moriarty's empire that had survived the eclipse of its founder.

Holmes' abilities as a fighting man were many. Apart from his knowledge of the obscure Japanese martial art of baritsu, he was a first-class swordsman and a professional standard boxer. In 'The Sign of Four' the retired prize-fighter McMurdo speaks of Holmes' abilities as a boxer, while Baring Gould in *A*

Biography of Mr Sherlock Holmes, the World's First Consulting Detective (Hart-Davis, 1962, Panther, 1975) says that the Holmes family spent two periods living at Pau in the south of France during Sherlock's teens and that it was during the second of these that Holmes studied fencing under Maître Alphonse Bencin, then said to be the finest swordsman in Europe.

CHAPTER FIFTEEN

The reference to the railway works at Swindon is, of course, a reference to the Great Western Railway's engineering works which were sited there. As to industrial workers making poaching expeditions into the countryside, on one occasion the apprentices of Huntley & Palmer's biscuit factory at Reading struck and rioted because two of their number were being hanged for poaching.

CHAPTER SEVENTEEN

The Coronation of Edward VII had been arranged for June of 1902 when His Majesty was attacked by appendicitis, necessitating an operation and convalescence. As a result, the ceremony was rescheduled for August.

Michael Harrison, in *The London of Sherlock Holmes* (David & Charles, 1972), devoted an entire chapter to an attempt to

254

work out which orders and decorations had been awarded to Holmes. After complex musings about such cases as 'the summons to Odessa,' 'the tracking of Huret, the boulevard assassin,' 'the death of Cardinal Tosca' and so on, Harrison suggests that the minimum list was:

From Britain:	Companion (Civil), the Most Honourable Order of the Bath
	Commander the Royal Victorian Order
	Order of Merit
	Companion, the Most Distinguished Order of St Michael and St George
From Sweden:	Grand Cross, the Order of the Seraphim
	Grand Cross, the Order of the Polar Star
From the USA:	Commander, Legion of Merit
From France:	Commander, Légion d'Honneur
	Les Palmes Académiques
	Chevalier, Ordre du Mérite Agricole (for his work at the Montpellier laboratories in 1894—see 'The Mystery of the Addleton Curse' in *The Mammoth Book of New Sherlock Holmes Adventures*

	(Robinson, 1997))
From the Vatican:	Cavaliere, Order of St Gregory the Great
	Commendatore, Order of the Holy Sepulchre
From Holland:	Chevalier, Order of the Marguerite
	Chevalier, Order of Orange-Nassau
From Turkey:	Chevalier, Order of the Medjidieh
	Chevalier, Order of Nishan-Iftikah
From Russia:	Order of St Anne (2nd Class)
	Chevalier, Order of St Andrew
From the Coptic Patriarchate of Alexandria:	Order of St George

Harrison suggests also that the 'King of Bohemia' in 'A Scandal in Bohemia' must have been a member of the Cassel-Falstein family and would have given Holmes the 'family order'—the Order of the Black Lion. He goes on to argue that Holmes had at least nine decorations or orders, probably nineteen, and, by 1920, might have had more than thirty.

Now it is amusing to imagine the elderly Holmes, if he ever left his beehives and 'dressed up' for a diplomatic occasion, festooned like a

Christmas tree with the jewels and ribbons of thirty or more orders but it is, with all due respect to Michael Harrison, highly unlikely.

Harrison stated that Holmes would not have held any British order of a rank higher than Companion or Commander, as the next step would have raised him to a knighthood, which we know he refused, but this is illogical. No one was more logical than Holmes, and he would not have set his foot on the lower rungs of a ladder that led to knighthood when he so strongly rejected that title. I think it is fair to say that, while he may well have accepted all of Harrison's list of foreign orders, he would never have accepted a British honour of any kind, and the present narrative—if it is authentic—reinforces that view.

Watson tells us, in *A Study in Scarlet*, that he qualified as a Doctor of Medicine in London, then took the one-year course for army doctors at the Military Hospital at Netley, Hampshire. The Royal Army Medical Corps had not then been formed and the Army Medical Service was a strange organisation, staffed by what were really civilians in uniform with officer status. Some were not even fully qualified doctors.

Netley Hospital was built on a grand scale, close to Portsmouth and Southampton, to receive the sick and injured of Queen Victoria's many wars, large and small. It was an enormous and decorative building set round an internal courtyard, on to which the windows of all the wards opened. Rumour said that the building had originally been designed for India and that the wards would have been less oppressively gloomy if their windows had looked on to a court lit by bright sunlight. Malicious legend said that the design had been intended as a palace for a friendly Indian Prince, but that the War Office had confused the plans and built the hospital in India while Hampshire got the Maharajah's palace. By World War Two it had become a white elephant and was gladly handed over to our American allies. They took one look at its ground-floor corridors three-quarters of a mile long and instituted an internal 'bus service' of jeeps circuiting the corridors to shift staff, patients and gear. It came back to British use for a few years (servicemen exposed to radiation in the Christmas Island nuclear tests were flown there for treatment in the 1950s) but in the 1960s it was shut down and then demolished. For all its shortcomings as a hospital, it is a shame that such an extraordinary example of Victorian architecture could not have been preserved.

CHAPTER EIGHTEEN

Devaux says that he was responsible for Theodore Trentham becoming the incumbent of Weston Tracey. It is the case that, for a long time, some parishes were 'in the gift of' the

258

local Lord, who appointed the parish priest instead of the Bishop making the decision.

The Thugs (the 'h' is silent) which means 'deceivers' and from whom we get our word for a violent criminal were a vast band of robbers and murderers who plagued India for centuries. The origins of this vile belief are ancient and unknown, but, as Devaux says, the centre of the cult was the worship of the goddess Kali or Bhowanee and it attracted men of many faiths. They would travel the roads and select a prosperous party of travellers. Joining them—'for protection'— they would await a suitable opportunity, then murder the entire party and steal their goods and cash, disembowelling the bodies and burying them in mass graves. For the legendary reasons that Devaux explains, they usually killed with a piece of cloth, weighted at one corner with a coin.

Despite the many thousands of murders which they committed, the East India Company, who administered India under a Charter from the British Crown, remained unaware of the cult's activities until the 1820s, possibly because the Thugs were protected by public officials, village headmen and even princes, all of whom took their share of the loot. W. H. Sleeman, an officer of the Indian Political Service (later Major-General Sir William Henry Sleeman, KCB), embarked upon a vigorous campaign against Thuggee, persuading many of them to turn 'approver' (informer), hanging many and transporting more until the grisly sect vanished. He believed that the sect had been responsible for a million murders. What we now know of the Thugs is largely derived from three books written by Sleeman, *Ramseeana, or a Vocabulary of the Peculiar Language Used by Thugs, A Report on the Depredations Committed by the Thug Gangs of Upper and Central India,* and *The Thugs or Phansigars of India.* There is also a book by Sleeman's grandson, Colonel James Sleeman, *Thug, or a Million Murders,* and a novel based on the testimony of a Thug 'approver' and written by an officer who had been involved in the campaign against the Thugs, *Confessions of a Thug* by Philip Meadows Taylor. While the Sleeman books are long out of print, Meadows Taylor's book was reprinted by the Oxford University Press in 1986.

Amorphophallus gigantum, the Titan Arum or 'Corpse-eating flower,' does not eat people, but it does exist. It stinks of carrion in order to attract the insects on which it lives. It was first recorded in 1878 by Dr Odoardo Beccari. By 1889 a specimen had been successfully brought to flower at Kew. Two years later, it bloomed again and a Miss Smith, an artist commissioned to draw it, suffered 'prolonged martyrdom that terminated in an illness'. Until a specimen in the Huntington Library Botanical Gardens, California, flowered in 1999, it had never been known to flower outside glass except in its native Sumatran forest. In the wild it can grow bigger than the specimen which Watson describes, the central spike or 'spathe' being as much as ten feet while the single leaf (which Watson calls a 'petal') can be seven feet across.

CHAPTER NINETEEN

Note the reference to a telephone at Baker Street. Central London had ten deliveries of post every day and Britain had a telegraph service which reached almost anywhere within minutes. Holmes was a frequent user of post and telegrams, but disliked the telephone and did not have one at Baker Street until 1898. When he retired to rural Sussex in 1903, he did without a telephone until the exigencies of his last case forced him to have one installed (see 'His Last Bow' and *Sherlock Holmes and the Railway Maniac,* Constable, *1994).*

'Chinese' Gordon was General Charles Gordon (1833–85). As a Second Lieutenant in the Royal Engineers he distinguished himself in the Crimean War and was promoted Captain. In 1853 he volunteered for service with British forces opposing the Chinese in the 'Arrow War.' In 1860 he personally directed the destruction of the Emperor's Summer Palace. In 1863 he became commander of a peasant force known as the 'Ever Victorious Army' which defended Shanghai against the Taiping rebels. Returning to Britain in 1865 he commanded the Royal Engineers at Gravesend while developing a mystical Christian philosophy and carrying out charitable work among poor youths. In 1873 the Khedive of Egypt made Gordon Governor of the province of Equatoria in the Sudan where he mapped the Upper Nile and established stations along it as far as Uganda. Made Governor-General of the Sudan, he crushed the slave trade and repressed rebellions before ill-health brought him back to Britain. After service in India, China, Mauritius and South Africa the British Government sent him to the Sudan to evacuate British forces from Khartoum in the face of the revolt of the Mahdi. Khartoum was besieged and, on 26th January 1885, the Mahdi's forces entered the city and Gordon was killed. A popular hero after his Chinese exploits, his death angered the British public, who blamed the Government for failing to support him. For reasons we do not know, Watson had two portraits in the sitting-room at Baker Street—one was General Gordon and the other was Henry Ward Beecher (see 'The Adventure of the Cardboard Box').

Sir Richard Burton (1809–81) left Oxford in 1842 and spent the next eight years in India. In 1853 he passed himself off as a Muslim to enter the sacred city of Mecca and in the following year was the first European to enter the forbidden city of Harer in East Africa. He led two unsuccessful expeditions to find the source of the White Nile and was the first European to discover Lake Tanganyika. He served as Consul at Fernando Po, Santos, Damascus and Trieste. He wrote more than forty volumes on his explorations and the peoples he had encountered and thirty volumes of translations including unexpurgated texts of *The Arabian Nights, The Kama Sutra* and *The Perfumed Garden.* His diaries and journals (and his last translation) were destroyed on his death by his wife.

Raja Brooke was Sir James Brooke (1803–68). A soldier in the service of the East India Company, he was wounded in the First Burma War and returned to Britain. In 1830 he travelled through the East Indies into China and in 1834 organised an unsuccessful trading expedition to the Indian islands. The following year he inherited his father's considerable fortune and, in 1838, sailed his armed yacht *Royalist* to the East Indies intending to create a settlement in Borneo. At Singapore he learned that the Sultan of Borneo was attempting to put down a revolt by the Dayaks in Sarawak. For his help in suppressing the revolt, Brooke was given the title of Raja of Sarawak which was granted in perpetuity in 1843. He explored the interior and did much to stamp out headhunting as well as establishing a stable government. In 1847 Britain made him Governor of the adjacent island of Labuan and Consul-General for

Borneo. He was eventually succeeded by his nephew, Charles Johnson, who changed his name to Brooke and became the second 'White Raja' of Sarawak.

Workhouses were the last resort of the aged, sick or unemployed poor who were no longer able to support themselves. They had a fearsome reputation for the harshness of their regimes and were universally hated by the poor but they survived until the coming of the Welfare State.

'Darbies' is rhyming slang meaning 'handcuffs' —a statement which looks a little strange. However, 'Darby's bonds' were a moneylender's bonds in the seventeenth century. Famous for being tight and grasping, Darby's terms were soon called 'Darby's bands,' as was anything that gripped and held. When rhyming slang emerged in the mid-nineteenth century, 'Darby's bands' became the term for 'hands' and later, by extension, for handcuffs.

CHAPTER TWENTY

For the occasion when Holmes and Watson passed a night, strait-jacketed, in a padded cell, see *Sherlock Holmes and the Royal Flush* (Constable, 1998).

'Sigerson' was the pseudonym that Holmes used while in Tibet during the Great Hiatus. There he passed himself off as a Norwegian explorer. Baring Gould, in the biography of

Holmes cited above, says that Holmes' use of the name was simply because his father's name was Siger Holmes, making Holmes 'Siger's son.' It is certainly the case that Norwegians had no legal surnames, as we know them, until 1908. Before that date they were always known as somebody's daughter or son, using second names like 'Piedersdottir' or, indeed, 'Sigerson.'

CHAPTER TWENTY-ONE

If the present narrative is really by Dr Watson, it clears up a longstanding mystery about his name. Although he styled himself 'John H. Watson,' he records that his first wife, Mary Morstan-Watson, sometimes called him 'James' and no explanation is given. Dorothy Sayers, in a deductive inference worthy of Holmes himself, pointed out that Watson is a Scottish name and suggested that his middle name was 'Hamish' which his wife had Anglicised into 'James' as a pet-name.

Paget was the artist largely responsible for illustrating Watson's stories in the *Strand Magazine* and establishing the most enduring images of Holmes and Watson.

The oleander is every bit as deadly as Holmes says; even honey made by bees feeding on oleander is poisonous. An Indian plant which now grows widely in Australia, the southern and western United States, Asia, Africa, Greece and Italy, it is known by a number of names, such as 'Jericho rose,' 'rose laurel,' 'rosa francesa,' 'laurier desjardins,' 'oleana' or 'olinana.' In Italian it is 'donkey killer' and in Sanskrit 'horse killer.' Although its deadly properties are well-known in the East, I can find it only twice in Western crime fiction (*The Piano Bird* by Lucille Kallen and *A is for Alibi* by Sue Grafton) and only once in Western crime.

The so-called 'King of the Western Crematoria,' former All-American football star David Sconce, was charged in 1990 with the murder of a business rival in the mortician's trade, Tim Waters, in 1985, by the application of oleander to his food or drink. Sconce had already been convicted of four counts of conspiracy to assault, three counts of grievous bodily injury, robbery, grand theft auto, receiving stolen property, four counts of removing body parts, two counts of mutilation of human remains, two counts of multiple cremation of human remains, two counts of commingling human remains and failure to inter human remains within a reasonable time. Another conspiracy to murder and many other charges were dismissed. He was sentenced to only five years. Although a preliminary hearing had ruled that he should be tried for the Waters murder, in 1991 the prosecutor withdrew the charge against Sconce as a result of complicating scientific evidence and inability to establish how oleander was administered.

There is also an American case of someone who died after being advised by a Haitian witch-doctor to use an oleander enema for slimming, and a (possibly legendary) case of an American Boy Scout who died after eating a sausage which he had roasted over a fire on a twig of oleander.

CHAPTER TWENTY-THREE

Death by lightning is relatively rare in Britain, but a small number of cases occur every year. Watson is right in observing that lightning kills when it passes through the heart. Electrical engineers are trained to keep one hand in a pocket while in the vicinity of powerful currents, so that any accidental shock will run straight down the body and not across the chest, a precaution said to have been first introduced by the great electrical scientist Nicola Teszla.

CHAPTER TWENTY-FOUR

There was a carpet woven for Queen Victoria by reformed Thugs. It may well still exist.

The superstitious practice of child sacrifice in India is authentic, and is presently on the increase.

Holmes' comments on brain damage and the peculiarities of the ears in multiple killers are astounding. The International Committee of Scientists to Study Episodic Aggression have identified a number of mental and physical indicators which are found in relatively high percentages of multiple murderers. One of these is deformed, lobeless, asymetrical or abnormally low ears; another is damage to certain areas of the brain by disease or accident. It is evident that Holmes was many decades ahead of them.

We know that Holmes retired in the autumn of 1903 and here Watson explains his reasons, but he gives us no hint of his own planning. We do know that he left Baker Street in early September 1902—that is, within weeks, if not days of the Weston Stacey investigation—and went back into medical practice at Queen Anne Street. It might have been both interesting and revealing if he had told us more about his own motivations, but then—he never does.

*   *   *

The foregoing, I hope, may assist readers in reaching their own conclusions as to the authenticity of this narrative. While nothing provides conclusive proof, I would draw attention to the fact that it comes from the same source as *Sherlock Holmes and the Railway Maniac* (Constable, 1994), *Sherlock Holmes and the Devil's Grail* (Constable, 1996) and *Sherlock Holmes and the Royal Flush* (Constable, 1998), each of which contains internal evidence strongly suggesting that it is an authentic work of John H. Watson. This is as entitled as they are to be accepted as genuine.